George P. McIntyre

The Light of Persia

George P. McIntyre

The Light of Persia

ISBN/EAN: 9783337291693

Printed in Europe, USA, Canada, Australia, Japan

Cover: Foto ©Andreas Hilbeck / pixelio.de

More available books at **www.hansebooks.com**

THE LIGHT OF PERSIA

OR

THE DEATH OF MAMMON

AND OTHER

...POEMS OF...

PROPHECY
.... PROFIT ....
· AND PEACE

TOGETHER WITH NEARLY THREE HUNDRED CITATIONS
QUOTED FROM

"THE LEARNED OF ALL LANDS"

*Which have a direct bearing not only on the Poems, but
upon the burning questions of the day*

By GEORGE P. McINTYRE.

CHICAGO:
THE WAGE WORKERS' PUBLISHING CO.,
1890.

" I have gathered a posie of other men's flowers,
and nothing but the thread that binds them together
is my own."—*Montaigne.*

No. 17.

ENCYCLICAL.

1818.

" The old earth reels inebriate with guilt,
And vice grown bold laughs innocence to scorn.
The thirst for gold hath made men demons!
Till the heart of him who feels the impulse of
    impartial love;
Nor kneels in worship foul to Mammon, is
    contemned.
The poor man's tears are unregarded,
And he whose righteous way departs from evil,
Makes himself a prey."—*Keats.*

PREFACE.

Herbert Spencer says the great superstition of the past was the divine right of kings ; the great superstition of the the present is the divine right of parliaments (legislatures). As the divinity of God kept the people poor the divinity of Government perpetuates the curse. It seems to me that all who advocate Individual Sovereignty should direct all their energies against the superstition of the State. All men agree as to the pernicious and corrupting influence of politics, but most of them look upon it as essential in the preliminary of government, which is necessary."—*A. L. Ballou.*

Is it at all surprising that the number of those who hold the opinion of the Church in light esteem should so rapidly increase ? How can that be received as a trustworthy guide in the invisible which falls into so many errors in the visible ? How can that give confidence in the moral, the spiritual, which has so signally failed in the physical? It is not possible to dispose of these conflicting facts as "empty shadows," "vain devices," "errors wearing the deceitful appearance of truth," as the Church stigmatizes them. On the contrary, they are stern witnesses, bearing emphatic and unim-peachable testimony against the ecclesiastical claim to infallibility, and fastening a convic-tion of ignorance and blindness upon her.—*Prof. Draper*.

" We cannot make people good by suppres-sion. If we would have superior characters, we must develop men's intellects, affections, conscience. We must so train them that it shall become a pleasure to them to do the right and shun the wrong. When people's minds are fully developed, they will do right of their own accord. They will not need to be con-stantly watched."—*Secular Thought*.

" The growing good of the world is partly dependent on unhistoric acts ; and that things are not so ill with you and me as they might have been, is half owing to the number who

lived faithfully a hidden life and rest in unvis-
ited tombs."—*George Eliot.*

" The economic questions now agitating
mankind are at bottom moral questions. The
right of property, for instance, is assailed.
The public teacher should examine whether
there is such a thing as a moral basis of property, and if so what that basis is. Laborers
demand a greater share of the products of their
labor. It is important to inquire whether there
is such a thing as a just proportion between
labor and the fruits of labor. The State is
called upon to interfere in behalf of the working classes. The vastly significant question
arises whether the State has moral functions
to perform or not, and if it has, how far it may
be justified in attempting to modify the economic conflict. Our moral teachers, if they
enter the struggle between laborers and capitalists as mediators without adequate knowledge of the subjects they attempt to handle,
will fall into deserved contempt. . . . .
" When it is considered how widely the religious beliefs of the past, with all the moral
checks and safeguards which they implied,

have been abandoned at the present day, it
cannot but be felt that a great danger threat-
ens our democratic communities in the absence
of any effective substitute for those teachings.
When we consider, on the other hand, how the
forces of conservatism are everywhere banding
themselves together to maintain reactionary
ideas, to keep the education of children and
students, the schools and universities in their
hands, we cannot but wonder that those who
desire progress should thus far have failed to
make any strong counter efforts to build insti-
tutions dedicated to freedom, as those others
are to authority."—*From the Proposed School
of Applied Ethics.*

"Good people who hold opinions not com-
monly understood, generally have a bad name.
The world is ready to believe almost anything
of a man except that he is a genuinely good
man. If his life is stainless but unconven-
tional, the world suspects some hidden shame
or base motive. So far are most people from
understanding or desiring what is true and
right that the highest truth is often believed
to be the lowest lie, and the purest right is
looked upon as the blackest wrong.

"Thus Jesus, who was the incarnation of earnest goodness, was said by the Pharisees to be possessed of a devil. That was because their own souls were so false that their moral visions were distorted. They looked upon goodness and thought it was badness. Thus also the early Christians were accused of indulging in lecherous orgies, when in reality they were living lives of great purity. It was only that they held unpopular doctrines; doctrines which most people did not, perhaps could not understand. Many persons understand their own selfishness, deceitfulness, greediness, and they cannot understand that there may be others who are unselfish, frank, and generous."—*Hugh O. Pentecost.*

"The men who most fear " Paternalism " in government have no dread of " Infernalism " of monopoly." —*W. H. T. Wakefield.*

DEDICATORY.

To the power that is behind Evolution, and to the author of the following poem, Mr. James G. Clark, whose manly courage I reverence and would emulate, and who, in my judgment, stands without a peer—the greatest living poet —the only one in these ultra-modern days of Shoddy, Creed and Cant, who has "dared" to voice in soul-stirring generalizations,* but nevertheless "in no uncertain language," the miseries of the poor; and to Georgina, my wife, sharer of my life's work, with joys too few, with sorrows too many, this book is tearfully, yet fearlessly, dedicated, in the hope that it may cause men and women to stop and inquire:

"Whither are we drifting?"

THE VOICE OF THE PEOPLE.

"Swing inward, O gates of the future,
   Swing outward ye doors of the past,
For the soul of the people is moving
   And rising from slumber at last;
The black forms of night are retreating,
   The white peaks have signaled the day,
And Freedom her long roll is beating,
   And calling her sons to the fray.

And woe to the rule that has plundered
   And trod down the wounded and slain,
While the wars of the Old Time have thundered
   And men poured their life tide in vain;
The day of its triumph is ending,
   The evening draws near with its doom,
And the star of its strength is descending
   To sleep in dishonor and gloom.

Swing inward, O gates! till the morning
   Shall paint the brown mountains in gold,
Till the life and the love of the New Time
   Shall conquer the hate of the Old.
Let the face and the hand of the Master
   No longer be hidden from view,
Nor the lands He prepared for the many
   Be trampled and robbed by the few.

The soil tells the same fruitful story,
   The seasons their bounties display,

THE DEATH OF MAMMON.

And the flowers lift their faces in glory
  To catch the warm kisses of day ;
While our fellows are treated as cattle
  That are muzzled when treading the corn,
And millions sink down in life's battle
  With a sigh for the day they were born.

Must the sea plead in vain that the river
  May return to its mother for rest,
And the earth beg the rain clouds to give her
  Of dews they have drawn from her breast ?
Lo! the answer comes back in a mutter
  From domes where the quick lightnings glow,
And from heights where the mad waters utter
  Their warning to dwellers below.

And woe to the robbers who gather
  In fields where they never have sown,
Who have stolen the jewels from labor
  And builded to Mammon a throne ;
For the snow-king asleep by the fountains
  Shall wake in the summer's hot breath,
And descend in his rage from the mountains
  Bearing terror, destruction and death.

And the throne of their god shall be crumbled,
  And the scepter be swept from his hand,
And the heart of the haughty be humbled,
  And a servant be chief in the land,—
And the Truth and the Power united
  Shall rise from the graves of the True,

And the wrongs of the Old Time be righted
    In the might and the light of the New.

For the Lord of the harvest hath said it—
    Whose lips never uttered a lie,
And His prophets and poets have read it
    In symbols of earth and of sky,
That to him who has reveled in plunder
    Till the angel of conscience is dumb,
The shock of the earthquake and thunder
    And tempest and torrent shall come.

Swing inward, O gates of the future !
    Swing outward ye doors of the past !
A giant is waking from slumber
    And rending his fetters at last,—
From the dust, where his proud tyrants found him
    Unhonored and scorned and betrayed,
He shall rise with the sunlight around him
    And rule in the realm he has made.''
                            —*James G. Clark.*

*The poems herewith presented aim to specify and
lay the blame for present iniquitous conditions where
they belong.

                            THE AUTHOR.

INTRODUCTION.

If the above term can partake in part, an autobiography in part, this, then, is an introduction.

That we have classes and class-privileges fostered by our system of government, no one, not even the most conservative, may gainsay. Recognizing the potency of the truism, that: "Revolutions come from above,"—it is the purpose of that part of this book devoted to Quotations, and, their arrangement in connection with my poems, to strengthen and reaffirm that proposition, and to prove that it is a "Mooted question" no longer; but that it is a fact in name, and in deed, and that here in these "United States" the boasted "Home of the free!" and the "Land of the brave!" that we have not freedom, and that we have not, as a nation, any bravery to spare; but, rather, that we are a nation of slaves, without bravery, without moral courage even to maintain what few rights are yet left to us as a people, and that we deserve not the name of freemen, and that now, as I write, we are in the midst of the grandest Revolution the world has ever experienced, and that we have not the common honesty and bravery to recognize its presence and make of it what it eventually will be, the kindest friend to the whole people, or the worst foe to the certain few. Recognizing also other truisms, that: "Real history is a history of tendencies and not of events," and, that: "Revolutions never go backwards," we are prepared to allay the fears of the timid, assuage the "cares" of the craven, and hasten to say, that, human nature can be thoroughly relied upon in this as in every other age.

Simultaneous with oppression comes the desire to redress the wrongs meted out to "poor weak humanity," and that this desire is perfectly natural, proves also that it is perfectly right, just and proper.

The greedy knave, and the cowardly slave,

have ever preached the " Let Alone" theory
until really *nice* men have come to speak of it
parrot-like, taking their ' Cue' from interested
parties who are " Eminently Respectable" and
are perfectly satisfied with *things* as they are.
To the latter class we have nothing to say.
But, to the *really nice people*, the leaders of
Sunday schools, etc., etc., the " respectable
middle class," and to all those 'hangers on' to
the ragged end of our so-called *society*—these
people who seem (?) to be totally unconscious
of the scorn and contempt they are subjected
to by that pre-eminently respectable class—
the satisfied, arrogant, haughty, the proud (?)
the vicious, base and mean, who demanded 36
per cent. interest for the use of their money
during our nations *need* (?)—these *imitators*
of vampires like-to-these, these really *nice*
people.—the doubtless holders of government
bonds from which they draw " comfortable
livings," these are the people with whom I
most desire an audience ; for they are the one
stumbling block in the way of all true progress ; but not for long, they will soon be called
upon to ' take a hand' in the impending ca-
tastrophy which will be sure to find them all

unprepared, because of their allegiance to the
" Laissez-faire."

It is the purpose of this compilation, together with the poems herewith presented, to
reach a solution to the constantly increasing
and most vexing question of capitalists and
laborers.

That each have rights, according to the in-
dividualistic theory, which the other is not in
duty bound to respect may not be gainsaid,
but who can deny, that a system which breeds
wrongs to whatever class, is totally wrong
and altogether unnecessary ?   It is with this
system as with an individual—" What you
are rings so loud in my ears that I cannot
hear what you say to the contrary."

It is generally conceded that Evolution is
no longer a theory, but that it is a cold, hard
fact beyond the power of controversy and
therefore wholly right because wholly natural:
and as through evolution the "Light" has
come to me, so will I impart that light in the
classification and arrangement of my poems,
giving the year, and, far as may be, the month
in which each poem was written, to prove that
by evolution alone I am, what I am.

Just old enough to "lug wood" when the civil war broke out, in which my father and three brothers took a manly part and served "during the war" with credit to themselves and honor to the nation: it will be remembered by thousands, that in the early stages of the war, "Uncle Sam" did not provide his "heroes" with money, and, dependent families suffered deprivations and hardships which are spoken of with pain to this day.

The screws of the money power were thus early fastened upon me: then came "flush times" almost before I was old enough to appreciate the meaning of them.

With little schooling, at thirteen years of age, I went out into the excitement of the times to "seek my fortune" but in reality to drift, drift, drift a creature of circumstance to which, save a period of five years, there has been no cessation, until, at times, I have been led to think that life was not worth living; and right here I want to state, that the suicides of the past fifteen years, have been creatures of my age.

The five years above referred to were spent in world wide travel, as a son by adoption, in company with a millionaire, who, were he alive to-day, would doubtless be of the *Laisezfaire* stamp, but who nevertheless " loved me dearly," so much so that he debauched my young life with examples of the " man of the world," encouraging every impulse of luxury, indo-lence and viciousness, but which terminated suddenly upon our return to New York after vainly trying to persuade me to marry his step-daughter, whom I could not love.

I speak of these phases of my early life to prove that through long suffering I have earned the right to say my say, and that my heart keenly throbs for my fellows. But, " I can always be stronger as myself than I can be as any one else."

We have no merit of our own in pleading,
    No grace of mind, no nobleness of heart ;
Soul leaps to soul, the Master interceding,
Imbues each man with strength to do his part.

Then will ye do it, ye men of " higher station, "
    Who draw your rations easily every day ?
If not, there is not room in all this fair creation,
    For some to live, who live, but never pay. "

                                        G. P. M.

Chicago 15th, January 1890.

FREE SPEECH.

"This is true liberty, when free-born men
Having to advise the public, may speak free!"
                              —*Euripides.*

"No greater calamity could come upon the
people than the absence of free speech."
                              —*Demosthenes.*

"Give me the liberty to know, to utter, and
to argue, freely according to conscience, above
all liberties."—*Milton.*

"To-day is so like yesterday, in cheats;
We take the lying sister for the same."
                              —*Young.*

"Thought in the mine may come forth gold or
        dross;
When coin'd words we know its real worth."
                              —*Young.*

" Hast thou no friend to set thy mind abroach?
Good sense will stagnate.   Thoughts, shut up,
       want air,
And spoil, like bales unopened to the sun."
                                        —*Young.*

" Speech ventilates our intellectual fire ;
Speech burnishes our mental magazine;
Brightens for ornament, and whets for use."
                                        —*Young.*

" The sun might as easily be spared from
the universe as free speech from the liberal in-
stitutions of society."—*Socrates.*

" In the body politic the spirit of freedom is
as the red corpuscles in the blood, it carries the
life with it."—*Prof. John Fiske.*

" The appeal of soul to soul is more potent
than law backed by majorities and standing
armies."—*E. H. Heywood.*

" Better a thousand fold abuse of Free
Speech ; the abuse dies in a day, but the denial
slays the life of the people and entombs the
hope of the race."—*Charles Bradlaugh.*

" I had rather be behind prison bars with the consciousness of having raised my voice in defence of downtrodden humanity, than tread the streets a free man (?) with my tongue bridled."—*Geo. P. McIntyre.*

"If you desire to better the condition of people by agitation, the first step is to assure yourself that you will not be denied the right to agitate ; to secure beyond a peradventure the uninterrupted exercise of your constitutional right of free assemblage, free speech and free press : yea, free as the winds of heaven, for less than this is not freedom."—An extract from a speech by the Hon. David Overmyer, delivered on Labor Day, at Topeka, Kan., Sept. 2d, 1889.

AGITATION.

The coward is afraid of agitation. The tyrant, the oppressor, the wrongdoer and the whole train of enemies to human rights and human prosperity fear agitation. The whole pack of obstructionists to progress are always ready to yell professional agitator when agitation begins to shake the foundations of error

and oppression.   Whatever progress the world
has made in the recognition of human liberty
and human rights, is the fruits of agitation.
Lovejoy was murdered while the mob screamed
that he was a professional agitator ; Garrison
was led through the streets of Boston with a
rope about his neck because he was guilty of
the "crime" of being an agitator.   Phillips was
hissed and rotten-egged because he would agitate ; a half a million of men were slaughtered
in our late war because it had been determined
to put a stop to agitation.   But the agitation
went on ; it fairly blazed over the grave of
Lovejoy ; it became hotter with every step that
Garrison took while in the hands of the mob ;
it swelled in volume as the eggs flew at Phillips ; it was taken up by new men and women
as Anthony Burns went back into slavery.   It
could not be stilled, for it was an agitation of
immutable truth.   That is the only sort of
agitation that troubles the world.   It never
finds fault with the agitation of error.   The
friends of error and injustice know that the
agitation will lead to victory and their down-
fall, just as sure as the sun rises and sets.—
Western Rural.

AGITATE!

" Come one, come all! this rock shall fly
From its firm base as soon as I !"

—*Scott.*

" Organization," cries number one.
" Co-operation," shouts another.
" More greenbacks," says the third.
" Moral suasion," bellows the fourth.
" Prohibition," feebly cries the fifth.
" Too much population," wails the sixth.
"Eight hours," says the seventh.
" Ethical culture," says the eighth.
" Strike," hisses the ninth.
"Dynamite," whipers the tenth.
" Overproduction," shouts the capitalist.
" Trust in the Lord," moans the parson.
And " Protection," yells the greatest robber
on earth.—*From the Remedy.*

" And, sir! is this not worth contending for,
to die for if need be ?"—*Hammond.*

Abolition of Wage Slavery.
Abolition of Private Property.
Abolition of Money.
Abolition of Poverty.

Abolition of War.
Abolition of the Legal Fraternity.
Abolition of Taxes.
Abolition of the Jury System.
And the establishment of the social equality of the sexes.

The sum of *Looking Backward.*

"Men of thought ! be up and stirring night and day !
 Sow the seed—withdraw the curtain—clear the way.
Men of action, aid and cheer them, as ye may !
     There's a fount about to stream,
     There's a light about to beam,
     There's a warmpth about to glow,
     There's a flower about to blow ;
There's a midnight blackness changing into gray.
Men of thought and men of action, clear the way !
     I come from the ether, cleft hotly aside,
     Through the air of the soft summer morning ;
     I come with a song as I dash on my way,—
     Both a dirge and a message of warning :
     No sweet, idle dreams, nor romance of love,
     Nor poet's soft balm breathing story
     Of armor-clad knights, at tournament gay,
     Where a scarf was the guerdon of glory ;—
Whistling so arily   Past the ear warily,
     Watching me narrowly,
          Crashing I come !"

                         —*Song of the Cannon Ball.*

" We do not take possession of our ideas but are possessed by
    them.
    They master us and force us into the arena,
    Where, like gladiators, we must fight for them."
                          —Heine.

YEARNINGS.

Hast thou to me a meaning,
O life of idle dreaming—
Always dreaming—ever seeming
    To be, what nothing is?
Is there no field of duty,
No aim—no wish for booty—
No secret, ideal beauty
    Inspired of life, as this?

All joys have I tasted,
Young years in pleasure wasted,
And hope is dead, or saited
    With life yet undefined—
Does aught remain worth seeing;
That would arouse my being
Into action, living, freeing!
    This yearning of the mind?

Is there no rule to measure,
This thirst disgusting leisure,—
No round of idle pleasure
    That one has not forgot?
Can'st tell me why this yearning
Life discovers, not discerning—
This inward, seething, burning
    To be, one knows not what?

Do'st know of one deep feeling;
The heart or mind concealing,

That would'st, by now revealing
    Allay this cursed pain ?
Is there nought in all creation,
That can by conjuration ;
Or by holy inspiration
    Awake to life again ?

O ! ye who groan with labor—
Who toil and growl at labor—
" Whose lives no pleasures savor (?)"
    This l-a-b-o-r would ye shirk ?—
Would I could change my being,
Into muscles tough, worth seeing ;
Into Nature-toughened-freeing !
    Gladly would I work.

Then rouse ye into action !
Into persistent action,
Disgrace no more your Saxon
    Tradition's, or its laws ;
" Be up ! and ever doing"—
" Fame comes with earnest wooing"
And to " keep the kettle stewing"
    Must be action before cause !

———

AN APOSTROPHE TO LUNA.

Thou southern orb of night !
    Thy disc of burnished gold ;

Blending silver in its light
  Subdues a jagged world,
And gives to it a beauty born of the Omnipotent.
  A chill to discontent
In mortals, gazing upon the night,
  Where splendor is revealed
In one harmonious light ;
  Becalmed, subdued, concealed—
From all but inward self ;
With pride ; the fiendish motor at its back
To urge it on and off the track
Of peace so yearned for
  In answer to prayer for light !
To shine forth upon the night—
Aurora's nucleus silent shines afar,
The myriad diamond-ray's of one great star,
  As shines the human heart, on earth, in heaven.
  What boots it then to mortals given
The right to peace on earth—
  The hope of peace in heaven ;
Where pride is not, where strife is not,
  Where all is light and beauty,
  And love is inward duty
    Freed from strife !
Freed from all the discontents of life !
  Freed from hopes blighted,
Freed from vow's plighted that broken be
  In our Halo of light,
   · ETERNITY !

THE PESSIMIST.

AD REFERENDUM.

"Hate the evil and love the good, and establish justice in the gate.   .   .   .   Let justice roll down as waters, and righteousness as a mighty stream."—*Hebrew Prophecy.*

"My child, you must not pick that rose or the man will cut your years off, and you must not run on the grass! Don't you see what it says on that board?"—*Lincoln Park.*

"It is because a few have got control of all the avenues of wealth, of all the channels of profit, and appropriated the proceeds of the labor of the many. They fence in every fountain, and bestride every stream and dole out the waters grudgingly, in small quantities, and for such services as they themselves shall command.—*The Voice of Labor, by David Overmyer.*

"Work on, do the work provided, whether work of brain or hand, as a "God-given task. Work, work, work; pray, pray, pray."—*Rev. Dr. Harris.*

———

The following stanzas appeared in the Chicago *Herald*, Sunday, March 20th, 1887 :

I live too much away from nature's own,
　　Its woods, its streams, its hills and cooling shades—
I would exchange the city's busy streets
　　For fields and flow'rs and emerald everglades.

The woods that spread their mantle over me
　　Spake peace as sweet as primal man has known ;
And I would be as free from guile as he
　　Whom God first chose to be his very own.

The streams that glide mid grazing pastures green
  Have, too, a tongue articulating low,
Which voice the soul with pebbled music sweet,
  And thrills with life the hopes of long ago.

The hills of hope high purpose gave to youth,
  Are still too high for wayworn feet to tread ;
And I would turn again to youth replete
  With hope as pure as though it were not dead.

The shades of life are manifold and deep,
  And shroud in gloom the glowing hopes of youth—
And I would turn to those refreshing glades
  My bare feet trod when hope was very truth.

The woods of life are circumscribed and bare,
  That once were vast, mysterious and wild ;
And boyhood's dream has turned to fell despair
  That man's estate and hope is but a child.

The streams of time are sluggish to the dip
  Of oars that lashed its surface into foam—
The strength of steam cannot some depths reveal
  That yield to chance from naught but surface loam.

The fields that yield their golden-weighted grain
  Are sheaved and housed by idle hands to-day—
No more it grows for him whose labor gains
  The sweat of brow, too oft his only pay (?).

The rose that blooms so fragrant on the lawn
  Is quite beyond these eager hands of mine ;

It, too, is chance to circumstance the same
  That causes much the ownership of time (?).

The air we breathe is but another tool
  To work for some unto another's woe ;
It, too, is worth so much per cubic foot,
  And brings its price with stifling overflow (?).

The light which streams up from the glowing dawn,
  That gilds the day for every mortal part;
It, too, is turned, perverted on its course
  To warm the soul, by brick and mortar art (?).

The laws of God, so binding on the poor,
  Are null and void unto the subtle rich ;
Whose paper floats exempt from taxes, all
  Evidence unknown, except to some poor wretch (?).

The pools that bask so smiling in the sun
  Too soon will roll in vapors overhead ;
The kine will come to slake their thirst in vain,
  And wondering gaze upon its empty bed (?).

And so to each and every creature thing
  Some good there is, but for some others more ;
And I would turn to youth and hope again,
  And flee the streets to some lone sylvan shore.

————

AGITATE !

TOO LATE.

" A begger in the wide world astray,
Knocked at a door the other day,
When another came forth to him and said :
'Brother of mine, proceed upon thy way;
To seek a shelter thou in vain art come;
Too many of us are here—there's no more room,—
The beggar was found a short way thence, dead.''

***

A powerful ruffian, you the folk oppressed:
The tyrant hung an order on your breast;
When as a traitor rumor branded you,
The stranger gave you order number two.
To-day a rebel to your former king,
Now from your button-hole new crosses swing;
But your crosses, chevalier,
Graveyard crosses all appear;
For every cross that glitters on your vest
Marks where a virtue died within your breast.
—*Translated for the Transatlantic.*

Against the frowning front of wrong,
He flung the ardor of his soul !
While mute beheld the craven throng,
Or owned, like slaves, the base control.
But bright on History's honored page
Shall shine the deed we spurn to-day ;
And men, in some heroic age,
Will own : HE BLAZONED FREEDOM'S WAY.
—*Francis M. Milne, in San Francisco Star.*

The following stanzas appeared in the Chicago *Herald*, Sunday, February 26th, 1888:

He who hath lived and left no word or sign
To tell posterity of his glorious youth,
When hope was at its full, and love and truth
Coursed through his veins, a tide of life divine,
Has missed the acme of his mortal part,
And filched from Him whose love was in his heart.

He who hath looked upon the face of day,
   Nor marveled at induction's high command,
   With God in all he views on every hand,
Nor felt a thrill that broadened all his way,
   Has missed the intent of existence here,
   If he leave no mark of value with his peer.

He who hath stood beneath yon starry sky,
   And, gazing on that canopy of gold,
   Nor felt the God within him so unfold,
Forgetting self in Majesty on High,
   Has missed the music of the mighty spheres,
   If he hath not praise to proffer all his years.

He who hath rocked upon old ocean's breast,
   Nor felt an awe steal o'er his inmost soul,
   Yet feigning, braved it to the distant goal,
Nor gladly leaped from off its foamy crest,
   Has missed the grandeur of its rhythmic swell
   If then he hath no marvelous tale to tell.

He who hath strained up to the mountain's peak,
   Nor wondering gazed upon that broad expanse,
   Nor dwarfed himself a pigmy in the lands
Unfolded to his view, with pallid cheek,
   Has missed the one thing needful to his fame
   If he hath not tongue to voice his Maker's name.

LE ENVOI.

He who hath scaled success with meed of opulençe,
   Nor shares it with his fellow whilst he lives,

Is base and mean.   Nor feels that to give
Is blessed, and knowing this, goes feigning hence,
   Has missed the purpose of his high estate,
   And will plead for mercy—but Too Late.

GREEEBACKS?   YES !

"Congress shall have power to declare war, . . . to coin money, . . . to regulate the value thereof."—*The Constitution.*

"To Coin—-to make money ; to originate ; to fabricate ; to coin as a word."—*Worcester.*

"Money was tendered to the government by Wall street banks ' at from 24 to 36 per cent interest.' "—*Appleton's Cyclopedia for 1861, page 296.*

"I affirm it is my conviction that class laws, placing capital above labor, are more dangerous to the republic at this hour than was chattel slavery in the days of its haughtiest supremacy."—*Lincoln's letter to Ellis.*

"O, war, thou fury of the past !
How ruthless thy conception cast
   Into the mould of greed and hate
   To wreck the proudest 'Ship of State'
That ever sailed upon the sea
Of commerce, peace, and liberty. . . . .
   History shall write thy cursed obliquity,
Thou monarchized, subsidized, bonded iniquity."
         —*From the poem Once a Year.*—G. P. M.

The leaders to that fearful strife,
   For sordid gain are leaders still,

Who wield the whip that smites the life
  In Freedom's name from vale and hill.

That life so vital to our state—
  Baptized in patriotic fire,
Whose zeal made soldiers truly great,
  Who scorn the party lash and hire.

That life is choked, and almost spent,
  From leadership of cravens greed,
Who dared to ask the "rate per cent"
  In answer to our nation's need.

Thirty-six per cent. by some was asked—
  I need not name the craven horde—
I leave to you the memory task
  ' For history verifies my word.

They, the leaders, self-anointed,
  Questioned long our vested right,
By the Constitution appointed,
  "To coin money in its might."

But we got it, soldiers got it,
  Sent it to their hungry wives,
Who paid their debts and learned to love it
  As they loved their very lives.

It was money, pure and simple,
  Honest money, green at that,
It climbed with gold and stormed the temple
  Of the world in its fiat !

Balked and beaten they the leaders,
   Strong united, (not over fond,)
But more to be feared than all seceders
   Were they who framed the government bond.

Bonds, they said, would save our credit,
   Bonds are made of paper, too,
Same as Greenbacks, but with debits,
   Added to their gilt-edged hue.

Greenbacks, they said, were "irredeemable"—
   What a lie their false tongues told !
And to me they are amendable ;—
   I preferred them to their gold !

I redeemed them—you redeemed them ;
   They redeemed themselves a million fold ;
By every hand they found redemption,—
   We preferred them to their gold !

Aye, they were a mighty power—
   A mighty leveler in the land—
They nerved the arm with which to shower
   Shot and shell with stronger hand.

They fought the battles of our nation,
   Crippled though as soon as made,
By gross "exceptions," strange negation,
   An apologetic coward's aid.

I need not recite the whole base story
   Of their withdrawal in redemption's name,

Nor how they issued bonds to worry
    And tax all labor in ludicrous shame.

I merely mention some "bug-a-boos"
    That cracked at the end of the party lash,
That did with coward fear infuse
    The rank and file of the " public hash."

Who shouted first, and last, and ever
    For " National credit" and " National banks,"
" Repudiation "—and that " Hard money measure,"
    " Intrinsic values" and " Resumption cranks."

" For overproduction"—under consumption—
    " Honest money"—the creature of law
Which could be twisted without compunction
    To mean anything which the leaders saw

Would hasten this creature into the fire
    That bonds might rise from the great ash heap
Which melted away, and was lost in the mire,
    Whilst the bonds remained with their interest deep.

He is her friend whoever dares
    Face her enemies with the truth,
With which to overthrow the snares
    Laid to entrap her growing youth.

He is her enemy—self-evident,
    Whoever partisan may be
That lets his party twist his bent
    For truth and its contiguity.

It is the leaders I charge to day
  Whoever led where wrong was wrought,
And not the rank and file, who pay
  For every wrong, however bought.

To every candid man of sense
  Contrasting the present with the past,
I make with him no vain pretense,
  But give an axiom that will last.

Let riches be not long despised,
  For it may come to every door,
Nor by its blandishments be surprised—
  It is a unit against the poor.

And when you see it strong arrayed
  On one side of a public cause
Then break with it, and be afraid
  Lest mischief come upon our laws.

The millionaires are leaders still !
  They led in piling bonds so high—
They are clipping coupons with a will
  And ask to be '' Protected''—why ?

'' Because they are the leaders''—'' leaders old'' !
  They lead in reaping but they never sow ;
They fix the price on all that's sold,
  '' And corn and wheat are always low.''

The inherent right is to ''sell to them,''
  '' A home market is just what we want''—

The market price you must ever stem
  No matter the price, however gaunt.

That ye are dupes self-evident !
  Witness the deeds of a "mutinous crew"
Who offered insult to a President—
  The Commander-in-Chief of "The boys in blue."

ALMOST A TRAGEDY.

" And shall I never have a home ?
  O say ! my fellows, say !
Is there no room for such as me
  In all America ?"—*Ingham.*

" Ah no ! not as now forever shall the eyes of Hope be dimmed
For Freedom's fruitless endeavor, and Labor despised and un-
    hymned,
For, lo ! even now a glimmer athwart the heavens above !
And hate and fear grow dimmer in the crescent light of love."
                              —*James M. Pryse.*

"Government is devised for the security of rights. The
rights of man are liberty and an equal participation in the com-
monage of Nature."—*Shelly.*

" I am sure there would be no need of laws to provide for
distress if there were no laws to produce it."—*Walker,*

" When all mankind were at war, every man who could carry
his club was worth his food. Peace has reduced this class to
starvation."—*Unity.*

I walk by homes of laughter, of music jest and
    mirth,—
But since the war I've had no home, there's none for
    me on earth—

My mother died, and father soon by her dear side was
    laid;
So now they have a glorious home 'neath heaven's
    umbrageous shade:
They earned it, too, in honest toil which never wrong
    has known,—
But when I came to live with them they then pos-
    sessed a home
Built by themselves, a dear old home, with maple
    trees around,
And oft, a boy in very glee, I've rolled upon the
    ground
And watched the swallows flitting by in twittering
    ecstacy,
And well I marked their sportiveness; it seemed to
    flatter me.
Oh! how I miss those dear dead days of peace and
    quiet joy,
And oh! the longings that I feel to be once more a
    boy,—
My elder brothers went to war to free the chattel
    slave;
And soon my father joined them—at sixty—he was
    brave !
I was a lad of eight years then—just old enough to
    share
The agony of dire suspense which filled our home
    with care.
No money came except I earned by driving cows and
    chores
That early morn and eventide I did about the stores.

A neighbor kind, who had a grove of beech and maple
    trees,
Gave me permission to "pick up sticks:" thereby we
    did not freeze;
But oh ! the toil of lugging wood so far upon my
    arms;
E'en most I feel them aching now, and see a war's
    alarms.
I could not earn enough for all, no matter how I
    worked,
And sometimes, yes, I know sometimes I cursed the
    war and shirked.
Dear mother sewed, and sisters too, but hungry oft
    were we;
And Sarah went away to live "wherever it might be."
Never before had one of us worked for a single soul,
Save those we loved about the home, and the larder
    was plentiful.
She did not tell a single soul her intentions thus to
    roam,
But bravely sought for work afar, that she might
    help our home.
O, did she know the agony of those she left behind?
Aye ! that she did, and speedily sent a message true
    and kind—
"I've found a place," the letter ran, "some eighteen
    miles away,"
"To sew for months; they seem so glad to have me
    here to stay."
She sent a greenback home to us, a new two-dollar
    bill;

The first that we had ever seen, and the tears would
    come and fill
Our eyes to o'erflowing so the bill was soon stained
    o'er
With spots, when we were kissing it—we all did thrice
    or more.
That bill—a "God-send" was to us, for I had stubbed
    my toe,
And we were hungry, and mother was sick, and
    everything seemed to go
All wrong, as sometime sure it will, till the black-
    hell-of despair
Was almost come unto our home, and angry words
    were there.
Those hot words, I recall them now—"I won't and I
    shan't!" I said
To mother, who wanted me to go to Simpson's for
    bread;
And I didn't, for just then Emma came from down
    street out of breath,
And brought the letter from "dear old Sate," which
    saved us all from death;
For I had resolved, let come what would, I never
    would "Borrow bread,"
And before I'd steal, as I felt I must, we might better
    all be dead!
And so a plot I laid to slay them all that very night,
But the letter came and saved my soul from that most
    awful blight.
This secret I've never told before. I hate to tell it
    now,

But boys are desperate as well as men, when hunger
    makes them vow,
Never to beg, and never to steal, yet never to hungry
    go;
They'd rather die like men ! than beg, or steal, from
    friend or foe.

THE MUSTER—A PROPHECY.

" Moreover, the profit of the earth is for all."—*Bible.*

"The earth hath He given to the children of men."—*Bible.*

" The land have I given for a heritage to all people."—*Bible.*

" The land shall not be sold forever, for the land is mine, and
ye are but sojourners with me."—*Bible.*

"Woe unto him that useth his neighbor's service without
wages, and giveth him nought for his work."—*Bible.*

The invisible hosts are marching in a cavalcade of
    might—
Hark ! I hear the clarion music ringing out upon the
    night—
And the seal of Faith now loosened is beneath their
    awful tread,
And the portals of the living are thrown open to the
    dead.
See ! A courier prone advances, swift as lightning in
    its wrath !

To muster all the sons of men to victory or to
    death !—
"Rally ! Rally !" is the tocsin message—welcome that
    he brings !
But he stops not !—yet he stays not !—on he flies with
    tireless wings !
But his voice peals as the thunder surging on some
    rocky shore,
And they hear it—aye ! they heed it—e'en the sons
    of men can roar !
Hark ! his trumpet now is sounding—"Gird your
    loins for the fight !
For a mighty army cometh to join forces with the
    Right !
See them coming ! Rally ! Rally ! from the North-
    land—east and west !
And the Southland brings her quota, larger now than
    all the rest ;
She who is opprest is coming to this carnival of strife,
She who is a maid or widow, she who is an honest
    wife—
All are coming ! none are fearing—yet they march
    with bated breath.
For they know, when all is over, they will be in at the
    death !—
God, I thank Thee ! it was given me thus to witness
    this array
Of thy power—in this the hour of our need and slow
    decay—
Faiths are quickened—pulses beating with that old-
    time ring and fire,

When men fought for homes and loved ones, for their
country and their sires.
But see ! the courier now returneth—giving out the
countersign—
"Down with Usury!" is the watchword, soldiers,
pass it 'long the line,
Yet again his his trump is sounding—" Muster every
man of toil !
Fill your ranks without a coward, to do battle for the
soil !
For to every man of courage will an angel ready be
To nerve his arm to strike a blow for homes and
Victory !"
They are with us, they are with us—they are here
upon the earth ;
They muster every kingdom to the places of their
birth !
I can see their banners swaying as they tread their
way among
The sons of every nation who have groaned beneath a
wrong ;
I can see the burnished armor gleaming 'thwart the
lightning's flare ;
I can read those bold inscriptions of past ages in the
glare ;
As they bring them back to witness here the wrongs of
long ago,
And to blend them with the scenes they find degrad-
ing here below ;
Ah ! they tell of pomp and power wrung from ignorance and youth,

Wrung from every timid creature who had innocence
    and truth ;

Wrung in Taxes, Tithes and Livings, wrung in monu-
    ments to the past,

By a horde of robber barrous who insinuated Caste,

See ! the toilers of past ages are in motion—drawing
    nigh,

They lead the van in marching—making way for Des-
    tiny !

I can hear the ring of metal whose keen edge is lost to
    art,

Fashioned into deadly weapons that can pierce the rob-
    ber heart,—

Hark ! a mighty voice is sounding—wave on wave it
    nearer rolls,

Hush ! it is the voice of Justice—having dominion over
    souls,—

List ye ! what that voice is saying—" Gird your loins
    for the fight !

" Death to traitors, robbers, harlots—death to every-
    thing—save Right !"

Tremble ! O ye sons of Mammon ! Tremble ! oh ye
    daughters, weep !

Who sell your birthright for an hostage, sell your
    bodies for their keep—

Hear that low deep-muttered thunder weiling up from
    off the sod—

(Given to mortals for an heritage—by its Creator and
    their God)—

Aye ! they shall have it—it is written—spoken now,—
    the written word,

And the gathered hosts repeat it—all may hear who
    have not heard.
Lo ! a mighty army marcheth, wheel on wheel the
    Legions sweep ;
Gathered from the inner fastness of the limitless and
    deep ;
Hosts are answering hosts and flanking—right and left
    they press around,
Here upon God's footstool gathered, to do battle for
    the ground—
Tremble ! O ye sons of Mammon ! Tremble oh ye
    daughters, weep !
Evolution now o'ertakes ye ; Revolution is its sweep !
Hark ! a mighty voice is sounding—wave on wave it
    nearer rolls—
Hush ! it is the voice of Justice ! having dominion over
    souls—
List ye ! what that voice is saying—"Gird your loins
    for the fight !
"Death to traitors, robbers, harlots,—Death to every-
    thing—save right !"
Hark ! the Leader's Voice is sounding—list ye what He
    hath to say,
He is calling to his children, and they must—they
    shall obey !
" Systems must give place to systems—Lo ! I come but
    not in hate,
"But to meet out simple justice—the advancement of
    the state !
He who will not aid endeavor to fulfillment without
    strife,

Must perforce in simple justice forfeit claims to Mammon's life !
Who has robbed of peace and plenty, robbed his fellow,
robbed the sod ;
Who so claims dominion over it yet shall feel the
wrath of God !
Lo ! I come to save my people—they with plodding
feet, and now
I am come to raise the lowly—they with careworn
aged brow,
They who toil in any vineyard, who have lived by
toil alone,
Are my children, blessed children—take the land, it
is thine own !"

AMERICA.

AN ADDRESS TO THE "AMERICAN HOUSE OF LORDS"
IN BEHALF OF THE "COMMONS."

"A Hundred Men with a Million a Year, ·
A Million Men with a Hundred a Year."

"This could not be if justice reigned."

" The gulf is widening between Dives and Lazarus at a geometrical ratio, and if this impractical society could possibly run

50 years longer, there would be ten men with a hundred million
a year and twenty million with nothing.   But it cannot last half
that time, for when millions of willing workers are hungry in
the presence of legally stolen wealth their respect for the law
evaporates."—*Looking Forward.*

> " So distribution should undo excess,
> And each man have enough."—*KingLear.*

———

"Want !" in a land of plenty—
 "Want !" did I hear you say—
"Want !" in a land of harvests!
 "Want ?" in America ?—
Great God ! and is it then true,
 That there is want in our streets to-day?
Gaunt want and wolfish hunger,
 And cold, in America?

Want ! in this land of plenty,
 Want ! in America,
Want ! where rivers of golden grain
 Are freighted far away ?—
Want ! where mast-fed swine
 Are roaming a thousand hills,
And mast-fed swine of another kind
 Are disconnting moneyed bills?

Want ! and the black diamonds sparkle
 In heaps a mountain high !
And some, perchance, must freeze
 In the streets, and perish miserably ?

Want! where idle treasure
　　Is piled a million's fold—
And is it Wisdom's measure
　　This hoarding of silver and gold ?

Must the living now go hungry,
　　When there's plenty wherewith to buy—
Oh say! must it be, ye Judges !
　　That from want, some of us must die ?
Must it be that the weak should go hungry
　　And cold, and thinly clad,
When the bountiful harvests yielded
　　Enough to make us all glad?

"The property rights are such,
　　"And the conditions of mankind so,
"It seems 'Divinely Right'
　　"That some must needy go;
"For in this struggle for life,
　　"The survival of the fittest—stand
"The Stewards of God's appointing
　　"To judge—of—the—case—in—hand.

"I know this seeme hard, my friend,
　　"But there's really no cause of fear;
"Just now, of course, money is tight;
　　"'T always is at this time of the year;
"Crops will soon move along;
　　"The farmers are much to blame;
"They've been holding wheat for a raise,
　　But they're mistaken, all the same."

Who gave you the power, ye Judges,
  Of want and plenty ? I'me told
By some, who are hungry and freezing,
  By some others who handle the gold.
Who gave them the power, ye Tyrants,
  To say that by gold alone
Or silver, perchance; bi-metalism;
  Shall be the measure of service done.

Who gave ye the land and the harvests
  Of cattle, of grain and of swine;
Who gave ye the land with its metal bright,
  And the coal in thè deep, dark mine:
Oho gave ye the power, ye Judges,
  To stamp on the metal bright;
"One dollar;" "In God we trust;"
  Does Power make everything right ?

Is Power the measure of Labor,
  Wrapped up in a small gold piece ?
Then am I the greater power;
  I can read it and melt it like grease.
Who gave ye the power, ye Judges !
  To measure my labor and skill
With coins that lie ! so miserably ;
  Do they do the "Master's will ?"

"Governments derive their just powers
  From the consent of the governed"—say
Is that the reason some starve,
  In the streets, or freeze, in America?

Ye Devils! ye Devils! who rule us,
  Who make of man's life a curse !
Who rob sweet innocence of virtue,
  Or debauch them with crimes that are worse !

Who make and unmake systems,
  To suit the will of the few ;
Who one day see danger in nothing,
  The next day prove it untrue;
Ye Devils ! ye Devils! who rule us,
  Who again are ruled by a crew,
Who in turn are ruled by the lust of gold
  And "The Press of a Foreign Jew."

Do ye think, ye Devils Incarnate,
  Who deed away lands by the mile,
That the hungry men of America
  Will submit to further guile ?
Do ye think that when want arises,
  And a vault that's groaning with gold,
That we will ask your consent to take it
  And pay interest a thousand fold ?

Do ye think when all is over,
  "And the music of praise is dead ;
"And crowns in the dust lie shattered,
  "That might have encircled your head,"
That the aftermath then waving
  Above the sordid few
Will have any the richer coloring,
  Because of the clodded dew?

If ye do, then keep on freezing,
    And starving the mad to-day ;
For there will come a glad to-morrow,
    When Mammon will slink away.
It moves along in majesty ;
    It is bearing down your way ;
Along the " Line of least resistance,"
    Right here in America.

EMBALM IT.

"Farewell ! a long farewell to all my greatness. "
                                —*Shakspeare.*

    " And then he did not stop, nor lag,
        But took within his reverent hand
        The starry emblem of our land.
    And kissed with sacred touch that flag,
    That precious, priceless, tattered rag. "
                                —*Helen N. Packard.*

" We are taught with our drawing breath that we should love
America and Americans better than any other land or people
Ah, yes. If it were not for that cry : " For God and Native land "
How would despots and plutocrats maintain their sway ?"
                                —October *Twentieth Century.*

$1.00.

        France has her lilly,
        And England her rose,
        And everybody knows
        Where the shamrock grows ;
        Scotland has her thistle,
        Flowering on the hill,
        But the American emblem
        Is the one dollar bill ;
                                —*Denver News.*

Sprinkle with spices and cedar
 And camphorgum, evenly, so;
Fold it up gently and neatly,
 That the stripes may all come in a row.

White stripes and red stripes alternate ;
 Fold upon fold it must lie,
Until each jewel that decks it
 Shines evenly through all the sky.

So fold it away for a season,
 For the stars of its glory are dim ;
No more does it tell the glad story,
 Nor the glass do we fill to the brim.

Waves it no longer for free men !
 It clings to the mast, there, in shame,
And the breezes that once kissed it with passion!
 Pass it by in utter disdain.

Waves it no longer for free men !
 It clings to the mast when apeak.
And looks tired and guilty —but maybe,
 If it had a tongue, it would speak.

It speaks to my heart, though, a language
 Whose muteness is born of the fire
Of freedom ! for freemen forever !
 And the appeal doth my courage inspire

To fold it away for a season,
 For its glory may sometimes return,

But until that glad day just embalm it,
   That traitors a lesson may learn.

*   *   *   *

When I was a boy, I remember,
   How my heart with emotion was thrilled,
When they brought home Malcom, my brother,
   Who at Malvern Hill was killed.

The flag of our Union was round him
   And he lay so calm and white
With a smile, as if Angels had kissed him
   For carrying that flag through the fight.

He got his death blow when the battle
   Was raging the hottest—it fell
From the hands of the colorbearer, near him,
   And he caught it up, and since then they tell

How it ever was seen in the vanguard
   Close up to the enemy, where
They mowed down his comrades about him,
   But the flag was invincible there !

He bore it though wounded and bleeding,
   Till the enemies guns were all still,
Then he planted it firmly and kissed it,
   And lay down and died on the hill.

His comrades all speak of him kindly,
   As a brave man and gentle and true ;

But he's gone with earth's glory around him,
Embalmed in the Red, White and Blue !

*   *   *   *

But no more does it wave over free men !
Though it set the black bondmen free (?)
For the " whites " and the "blacks " are bonded
To a fell-money-curst Oligarchy !

So fold up the flag for a season :
The days of its glory are fled ;
It is now with the Heroe's departed,
And its wrong to mock even the dead.

So sprinkle with spices and cedar,
And camphorgum, evenly, now
Embalm it and pledge yourselves solemnly—
By the most sacred and awful vow :

" By the gods of Reason and Justice !
By the cramps of Hell and its blight,
The earth shall be deluged in blood,
But that Right shall rule over Might !

" That the flag we embalm for a season
Shall exultingly wave from on high !
A beacon to earth's weary mortals,
And no more be a jest and a lie !

That again it shall float over free men ;
Stripe upon stripe it shall wave—

An emblem of glorious achievement—
  O'er the homes of the free and the brave !

Then rally ! The peaceful solution
  Must be tried and fearfully prest,
Till we fail in our efforts to rid us
  Of this trust-given reign—then the West

An army of brave men must gather,
  That shall sweep in its maddened glee,
All " trusts " and those Hellish land-grabbers
  Of " Protection " out into the sea !

So cover it deftly with canvas,
  Hide the " Blue Jack " from my sight,
It's " forty two stars " a misnomer,
  There's no Union if " Protection " be right !

Aye ! cover it deftly with canvas,
  Cement it the mumified !   Now
'Tis embalmed.   Renew your pledge solemnly
  And carry out your most awful vow.

THE TREE OF STATE.

" The people are the roots of the State ; if the roots are flourishing the State will endure."—*Chinese Maxim.*

" The relations of structure are actually such, that, by the help of a central regulative system, each organ is supplied with blood in proportion to the work it does."—*Herbert Spencer.*

"Is not a dollar a day enough to buy bread? Water costs nothing, and a man who cannot live on bread and water is not fit to live."—*H. W. Beecher.*

"The time is near when they (the banks) will feel themselves compelled to act strongly; meanwhile a very good thing has been done; the machinery is now furnished, by which, in any emergency, the financial corporations of the east can act together at a single days notice with such power that no congress can overcome or resist their decision."—*The New York Tribune.*

———

"The roots of the State"—are they flourishing?
    Does each fiber receive its just share
Of that sapient food, which is nourishing,
    To keep them from hunger and care?

"The roots of the State"—are they flourishing?
    If so, then the "State will endure,"
For the blood that flows free is all searching!
    And each trivial ailment will cure.

But the "roots of the State"—are they flourishing?
    Does each ligament receive a supply
Of that life-giving tide so encouraging
    That each fibre of State cannot die?—

"The roots of the state"—What are they?
    Are they scions, or grafts of "The tree
Of State" we all (?) speak of so boastfully
    We call it: "The home of the free"?

"'The roots of the State' are its people."
    To be healthy, each scion should be

Well housed, well fed and be equal
    In the sight of all state equity.

"The roots of the State"—are they healthy ;
    Does the soil cling close to each root ;
Does each fiber grow strong, and abundantly
    Able to support a new shoot ?

Is the State we boast of, so vauntingly,
    Prepared to affirm that the pay
Each growth receives, and that, tauntingly,
    Is enough at "a dollar a day ?"

That life-giving tide in all nature
    Animate, or inanimate as well,
Be it sap, or the blood of a creature,
    Or the State circulation, must tell

On the strength of the Tree and its branches,
    For its roots will wither and die ;
If an ax be sunk deep in its haunches,
    And its life tide be sapped until dry.

The National Banks are the axes
    Sunk deep in our proud Tree of State !
Suborning all law, which, relaxes
    In relieving the "cares of the great."

Discrimination, with its vulgar sequences,
    Have debauched the life of the Tree,
Until Justice is blind and enhances
    The work of all mean deviltry !

Great God !   What a state are we in !
    The poor have no show with the rich ;
They have not the wherewith to begin
    A suit to recover, the which

They have toiled for—and lo, the reward,
    And to get it—Ah ! that is the rub,—
They are given a piece of pasteboard
    Payable ten years hence—but, in blood !

Can we expect a healthy State-tree,
    Or a man to be strong in the State
When the blood of his own liberty
    Flows flush through these Entrails of hate ?

Is it wisdom to longer entail
    These leeches upon our fair State
Till a premium is put upon " gall,"
    That is flushed with the jaundice of hate ?

" For the rich hate the poor"—and in turn
    Are hated with the blight of a curse !—
But the rich can—afford—slow—to—burn,
    So long as they have not to disburse.

And " the banks can act strongly," they say,
    " With but a day's notice ahead ;"
They can bring about worse " anarchy"
    Than when " Justice" with murder was fed !

They have preached " Gatlin guns for the mob !"
    Who in turn have recourse to the curse ;

They hurl in the deadly bomb,
　　And I know not which side is the worse.

In the light of time's—search—evidence,
　　One cause was to blame, it, the "purse!"
What language of mine can evince
　　My contempt for it and the curse

It wrought to that fair, hallowed Tree,
　　Around which my heart-strings entwine ;
'Till now, I no longer can see
　　But that Anarchistic-Justice combine.

Poor thief ! it "robbed Peter to pay Paul,"
　　And now the "black devils from Hell"
Have full sway in the courts, one and all,
　　And I mark me, the Tree is not well !

Avarice—the grub—is at its roots
　　They are into another "combine !"
The disease has seized all its shoots
　　But they drink but the froth of the wine.

Yes, the Tree is unwell, this I know—
　　'Tis decidedly weak, but, I am loath—
The remedy to heal startles so ;
　　It would shake off this incubus growth.

But I fear, with a fear born of love ;
　　Which no man shall dare under rate,
That it will take millions of tears to remove
　　This Octopus leech from the State !

Yes ! I fear, I repeat, with a love
    For my fellows both humble and great,
It will take thousands of lives to remove
    This grub from our fair Tree of State !

THE GROOMING OF THE GIANT.

" The most wealthy must govern in every state, and will, regardless of any attempt to deprive them of that right."—*Richmond (Va.) Whig.*

" We need a strong central government ; the wealth of the country has to bear the burdens of government (?) and shall control it."—*Senator Sharon.*

" It is the business of governments to " protect" the interests of business men and they in turn will look out for the poor."—*President Garfield.*

" The only way we can control the working man is to make him eat up to-day what he earns to-morrow."—*Tom Scott.*

" Hand Grenades should be thrown among those who are striking to obtain higher wages, as, by such treatment they would be taught a lesson, and other strikers would take warning by their fate."—*Chicago Times.*

It is coming ! It is coming ! Lo ! I warn you to be
    ready !
Place your chemicals in fusion, let the bulbs receive
    the air ;
For the hope of all the ages is concentered in this
    struggle,
And you must not waste a moment, not e'en to make
    a comment ;

But be ready with the weapons Science kindly has
    provided
For this very undertaking though it end in death to
    you—
Though it end in black death freezing some-one-else
    instead of you—
They have built upon your loyalty a fabric of base
    cruelty,
And now you'll shake it off and stand, or fall with
    honor true ;
True to self and true to duty, true to brotherhood and
    beauty ;
True as God Himself intended you should be to all
    the race
Else be branded as a traitor—a base and craven traitor !
And be driven hence like cattle to the shambles in
    disgrace !
I can see your lips draw firmer and your countenance
    grow sterner ;
As I tell-you-off in language that is plain and under-
    stood,—
You have mixed a life of sorrow from necessity of labor
And you've borne it long in secret and are longing to
    be free !
Long to shake-off every fetter which enchains your
    liberty ;
Long to recognize your manhood or go hence eternally !—
The bonds of superstition which for centuries en-
    slaved you ;
Were broken in transferring them to bonds of gov-
    ernment,

But the change, though somewhat better, is insulting
    your intelligence ;
And that, too, is doomed to scatter 'neath the wrath
    of your contempt.
Yes ! the animal that's in you cries aloud for readjust-
    ment ;
Of conditions all unnatural and you've made a solemn
    vow,
That when the time was fulling it would find you keen
    and ready ;
To strike a blow for vict'ry and strike home ! or failing,
    die !—
'Tis a battle of the giants !   This you know and long
    have measured
The strength of your opponent all entrenched behind
    the law ;
But the "Court of Last Resort" you rely upon for
    judgment,
So you've trained your mind accordingly and will not
    now turn back.
Not though grim-death this moment stared you in the
    face and giggled !
Would you turn aback to struggle in the old degrad-
    ing way ;
But would set your teeth the firmer, and grind them
    too and murmur
"Come death," "Come sweet oblivion," or "Come
    Victory and life ! ! !"
No coward you, nor craven, nor a sluggard, nor a villian ;
But you've been an honest citizen and you could not
    " get ahead ;"

In the struggle for a living,—just barely for a living
You have grown old and grizzled and have horns in
    neither palm—
But they'll grip the ax the tighter, aye ! and grasp
    the bomb the closer,
And the arm that's trained to labor will prove your
    staunchest friend ;
For although it prove quite sanguine—'twill be a san-
    guinary struggle,
So you fear not the result, for which, you are ready
    now to die.
You will prove an honest foeman—no contemptible
    assassin ;
You will give your foe a warning like the " Rattler
    ere he strike,"
And the " Gatlin's" they turn on you—you will
    bomb them into silence,
Then form an armistice with them, till they strike
    again at you ;
Whereupon you'll end the struggle by entire anni-
    hilation
Of your enemy, the liar, the craven and the cur !—
Thus will labor gain a Victory over Capital—thus only
Will the elements composing each be " Harmonized"
    for good ;—
It will be a lasting lesson which will hasten the mil-
    lenium,
For the good of all the ages ever came up through
    some blood ;
Thus through cooperation will advance man's brother-
    hood ;

Thus the dream of all the ages will advance the perfect day,
And "The Stage-coach," with its "Drivers," will forever roll away.

.

THE LIGHT OF PERSIA.

" Zeal and duty are not slow,
But on occasions forelock watchful wait."
—*Milton.*

"Sired of ye Sun and mist,
    Foal'd in ye angle of might !
Caught in descent, how ye hissed
    Ye liquified devil of Light !"
—*Cibler.*

"Think you that a drop of water, which to the vulgar eye is but a drop of water, loses everything in the eye of the physicist, who knows that its elements are held together by a force, which if sudddenly liberated, would produce a flash of lightning ?"—*Herbert Spencer.*

It can be stored in a small wand, which rests in the palm and, when skillfully wielded, can rend rocks, remove any natural obstacles, scatter the strongest fortress and make the weak a perfect match for any combination of number, skill and discipline. " —*The Coming Race : By Bulwer.*

I come ! I come !—ye have called me long :
I come o'er the mountains with Light and song !
—*Mrs. Hemans.*

Hail ! all hail ! Thou light appointed—Hail thy coming at this hour ;
Hail thy quickening conservation to dethrone the money power.

We thy servants long have waited, long have strug-
 gled, long endured ;
But the knowledge of thy Presence much our patience has inured,
Wrapped in mystery, song and legend, thou hast
 tardy been,—but say !
Now we fully have possession—SCIENCE bids Thee
 ever stay !—
And caus't thou now our animation full suspend till
 time is nought ;
And by that mystery so potent has't thou a quickening antidote ? ?
If thou hast, the test on yonder flock of sheep may'st
 fully try ;
For if thou fail'st to reawaken, they are but sheep !
 as such, may die.
Quick the mysterious power hovered o'er the flock
 and then it fell ;
And had that flock been Bankers, Lawyers, they had
 been "pleading" now in hell !
For, to attest the strength of vapors, thus exhaled
 from small glass bomb ;
Investigation was suspended, with proof enough to
 strike one dumb !
And so that flock of sheep are standing staring into
 empty space ;
Some whose bleating breaths were frozen, others
 stopped in gambols chase ;
Others still with lambkins nursing, others yet with
 grazing mouths ;

To the sward their heads are drooping, others still
    their nostrils souse.
Ah! Thou Glorious "Light of Persia," thōu art
    here, art come to stay!
Yes! thou'rt with us to be useful, and to claim the
    "Right of way!"
Heretofore the railroads claimed it, hurtling death on
    either hand;
And by functions usurpations stole the public's
    wealth of land :
Lied and robbed, subborned and plundered, denying
    usucaption's right,
Despoiled the farm and then the farmer scourged his
    home as with a blight,
Then with fear of revolution, craven fear of steaming
    blood;
Allied to "Courts of prostitution" (builded for the
    people's good) (?).
And so appealed to "Patriotism;" that wrecker of all
    moral law;
(That bane to homes; a nation's curse; that monster
    with a cat-like paw!)
To yet oppress and grind the "public" to see how
    much it could endure
Till marriage even was denied to some who waited
    years and more.
And when the discontented murmur swelled aloud
    and strikes were " on ;"
They struck men down-with-anarchy and threatened
    with a Gatlin-gun.

The "blood" possessed of so much "horror" was
    not the people's, their concern
Was for themselves; they quaked and trembled, for
    themselves their morals burned.
But now we'll force the revolution, no harm in one
    whose bloodless might,
Sweeps the land with noiseless power, sweeps it with
    the power of Light !
Who can tell the brave "Light-bearer" as he treads
    the busy street,
Who but they can tell the hour when the allied forces
    meet—
At noon, upon a given day the pampered works of all
    the world,
Will silent be, as noiselessly the planet in its course
    is whirled;
No questions will be asked, "for why," from dread of
    the impending doom;
The earth will quiet be as erst, upon that day from out
    the gloom
It rolled into the quickening light, when day was
    ushered into night.
Men will be mute and quit their work and hasten
    each upon his way;
He has a duty to perform—a duty? Yes! upon that
    day.
He knows his task yet dreads it not, for he is master
    of his fate,
His only fear, if such it be, is, that he may not be too
    late:

For he has pledged his right to life if thus he fail to
    do his part,
And the forfeit will exactly be from every traitor's
    craven heart.
His part is simple. In his right hand he holds a
    globe of "Instant Light,"
So small is it, that his good palm conceals it from his
    fellow's sight.
A hundred thousand such as he, could withstand the
    armies of the earth,
He knows it, too, and fearlessly joins the ranks to aid
    the birth
Of a new regime, for "fallen man." The Christ of
    history foretold,
When he would come, and willingly, undo the misery
    of gold.
He came but no one saw Him come; God moves in a
    mysterious form,
"He plants his footsteps on the sea and rides apon the
    storm,"
"How resist this revolution?" Ah! die you hard
    thou guilty wretch!
Mammon takes no note of Science unless it will itself
    enrich.
"How arrest the revolution?" will be heard on every
    hand that day;
Mammon dies; but dies from hunger; because it will
    no longer pay:
Yes! it dies. But in its throes 'twill call upon its
    henchmen brave (?)

Who will be willing for a shilling yet its guilty life to
    save;
Henchmen who are blind to reason, blinded with
    obsequious gain,
So in Godless doubt and treason they must pay for it
    in pain.
Yea, they will face the unknown power—hireling
    troops of Mammon's gold,
And they too must agony suffer, suffer from the biting
    cold;
That sweeps like magic o'er their forces, creeps in ter-
    rorizing blight,
As cold their veins, benumbed to freezing, from the
    contact of the Light !
"How resist the revolution?" "Suspects" may go
    to jail in peace ;
Knowing well at any moment they can "treat" for
    their release !—
The court-room's thronged with zealous faces—the
    prisoners—so—behind the bar ;
The judge his sentence has delivered,—Presto ! the
    Light is there !
The judge, the jury and spectators have met "suspen-
    sion of the breath !"
A capsule in the prisoner's mouth frees him from the
    frost of death ;
And forth he walks a conqueror triumphant o'er a
    natural cause,
That bids defiance to the courts and all their base,
    inhuman laws.

    *   *   *   *   *   *

But the pot ! the pot ! the horrid stink pot ! the stink
    pot of Egypt old !

In mercy is sent to these slayers of men who ,knew
    but the mercy of gold.

With gaspings and sneezings the antidote works, the
    crowd revives from the spell,

The Light of Persia subjected them to, but they sigh
    for a continuance of hell !

And in their mad scramble for a breath of fresh air
    they mangle each other in strife,

And some perchances perish who never can tell the
    test of the pot over life.

Will the judge, and the jury, and the bloodthirsty
    crew who clamored for the death of "suspect,"

Be content with the lesson they scrambled to get and
    prove to the law derelict?

Will they see, will they learn, that the laws of the
    courts are null except but for good ;

That the "court of resort" invested in man is a gift
    to the whole brotherhood ?

Will they see, will they learn, that man's intellect col-
    lectively based upon right,

Will never submit to a rule that is mean and con-
    temptible in their their sight ?

Till they do, the glad Light of Persia shall shine to
    confuse and confound every law,

That is not based on justice and true equity to which
    the whole people may bow.

Then hail ! all hail ! thou secret of old ! thou limpid
    quintessence of Light !

Thou friend of the masses most potent for good though
    death frigid lurks in thy might,—
Do they think to enslave Thee, or thy antidotes learn,
    do they think Thou too art for sale ?
Can they buy the whole earth with a portion of it, can
    they buy all the right of entail ?
Do they know that the Bearers of Light only know
    their kind in the craft strict appointed ?
Do they know that the stink-pot bearers don't know
    by whom they themselves were anointed ?—
Do they think there's a loophole for Pinkerton men,
    though they number the leaves of the trees ?
Well, there is, but that "loop" is connected with
    death ! There's no antidote for any of these !
Then Hail ! all hail ! Thou Transpicuous Light !
    Thou essence of Permanent Good !
We welcome thy power, acknowledge Thy Right to
    Rule over man's brotherhood.

THE ANSWER.

    " How is it.   .   .   .   through all these years you
    Have remembered me."—*Mallock*.

    "Is it possible that I am remembered upon that brief, but
    joyous occasion ?"—*Private Letter*.

    "We met, 'twas in a crowd. I thought that he would shun
    me."—*Old Song*.

    What is love ! It is something that I feel, that moves me,
that gives me joy, that tends to keep me pure and good. It is
something that I experience toward this person and not that. I

love my wife not because she is beautiful or homely, or bright or dull, or tall or short ; and I love my friend not because he is this, that or the other. In both cases it is because there is something in my wife and my friend that awakens my love. But I cannot explain my love to you. I can only say : "Were you ever in love ? Then you know what love is."—*Hugh O. Pentecost.*

"I hold he is best learned and most wise :
Who best and most can love and sympathize."
—*From the poem* "*Wisdom.*"

———

The following stanzas appeared in *The Current*, May 29th, 1886 :

We question not in spring-time
 The budding of the trees,
Nor warbling of the songsters
 Their varied melodies.

We question not the sunshine—
 We question not the rain—
We question not the flight of time,
 Its joyousness or pain.

We question not the river
 Which flows on to the sea—
But accept each from the Giver
 Of boundless charity !

Then question not that fullness
 My friendship has for thee ;
' Tis mystery full as infinite ;
 As Infinite mystery.

We met not, then, as strangers;
  Met we not then as friends?
ᵥ Mysterious mystery lingers---
  Affinities have not ends !

And like all else in nature,
  We take a royal part.
There's soul in every creature,
  Who has a loyal heart.

THE APPEAL.

My friend—come now, and succor me—
  For, I have "err'd and gone astray—" (?)
But, 'tis on the side of humanity,
  And so have not gone far away:
But, lest man's proneness to condemn;
  Should malice bear and vengeful spite—
Thy Poet heart will not contemn,
  For thy sake, too, I make this fight.
Come, speak! and vindicate thy friend!
  The fight he makes must not now, cease—
Come bear him out—Thy message send
  Throughout the earth, nor speak of peace
Until the last Mammon's race,
  Have met the Master face to face!

AGITATE !

TRUE MEN.

God give us men ! A time like this demands   ,
Strong minds, great hearts, true faith and ready hands,
Men whom the lust of office does not kill,
Men whom the spoils of office cannot buy,
Men who possess opinions and a will ;
Men who have honor, and will not lie ;
Men who stand before a demagogue
And damn his treacherous flattery without winking !
Tall men, sun-crowned, who live above the fog
In public duty and in private thinking ;
For while the rabble, with their thumb-worn creeds,
Their large professions and their little deeds,
Mingle in selfish strife, lo ! Freedom weeps,
Wrong rules the land, and waiting Justice sleeps !

WHY IS THIS ?

When the land is full of workers,
    Busy hands and active brains,
When the craftsman and the thinkers
    Feel about them binding chains ;
When the laborer is cheated
    Of the work his hands have wrought,
And the thinker, vain of logic,
    Sees that reason comes to naught ;
When the forces men have harnessed
    And have trained to do their will,
Ought to leave no homeless people

And no hungry mouths to fill,
Have but proved themselves the servants
Of the shrewd and selfish few,
And the many have but little
For the work they find to do ;
When the labor of a million
Goes to swell the gains of one.
As the serfs ef ancient Egypt
Starved beneath the burning sun ;
When the schemer and the sharper
Hold the wealth and rule the land,
Using up the thinker's brain force,
Mortgaging the craftsman's hand ;
When the many shear the sheep
And the few secure the wool,
And the gallows claims its victims,
And your costly jails are full :—
Then the men who dreamed of progress
And had hopes of peace and bliss,
While they weep and wonder vainly,
Ask each other ; "Why is this?"
Then he thinks, while confessing
That his vision yet is dim,
Say, that one thing, very clearly,
Is apparent unto him,
That the people, blind, or heedless,
Place themselves beneath the rule,
Either of the fiendish knave, or
Worse, perhaps, the sodden fool."

AGITATE !

POVERTY.

"I come !   I Come !—Ye have called me long :
  I come o'er the mountains with Light and Song !"
                                  —*Mrs. Hemans.*

I come!   I come!   I must no longer stay
  From duties keen reproach at lingering here;
Else rust shall gnaw my vitals all away—
  Yes ! go announce—I shall ere night appear !"
                                  —*Ivan S,——*

———

There is a sullen artificial sea
With breakers lurking near each murky wave,
Fix'd there by the mean avaricious knave
Whose coral home, call'd "The Land of the Free,"
Is made of shipwreck'd mortal's misery.
The drowning wretch he seeketh not to save,
For soon the sufferer becomes a slave
To serve him in "The Land of Liberty."

The marines are the despised poor,
Whose loved one's lives to them are just as dear
As the belov'd in coral homes secure.
This free man's bondage is the most severe.
Knaves with white liver say their blood is bluer,
Then eat his bread, and thank him with a sneer.

———

AGITATE !

THE TOCSIN.

Signals of storm o'er the lakes and the land;
   Flashing of steel and flashes of brand;
Ringing of helmets and grinding of knife;
   Gaunt labor calling his children to strife!
      Form! Form! Workingmen, form!
      Ready! get ready, to meet the Storm!

The tyrants are forging their bay'nets anew:
Who are they for, if they are not for you?
You who, impotent, have weakened your chains?
And hark!   They are driving the rivets again!

Thousands of years they have trampled your blood;
See, it reddens the fanes of their old money god!
What is the outcome but honor and shame?
What your rewards but a rod and a flame ?

They are building a gallows new lessons to teach!
They are hanging your brothers for freedom of speech!
You are held to your tasks by praetorian gun!
You are clubbed if you halt and shot down if you run!

"Honest," they call you while peaceful you dig;
Honest! content to live like a pig;
Honest! your daughters they curse with a stain
That blisters your lips to give it a name.

Honest! your sons their prisons to fill!
Honest! your aged their pauper dens kill!

Honest! your babes to the sinister floods
Which shelter and fatten their crocodile gods!

Lo, you! upon the bright breast of the west
A fortress! A menace, your courage to test!
Thus your petitions are answered; their jeers
Are fittting replies to your whines and your tears.

Our bravest, our truest, our best are in chains.
Shame to the watery blood in your veins!
Starvlings of honor and curses of earth!
Proud of your copper badge-sign of the serf!

Doff it! Who 'mong ye are freemen, free born;
Resolve! and the cities in sackcloth shall mourn
The day! Let their bastiles go down in the morn
While the flames of your wrath mock the red of the
        dawn.

Now form ye by ones, or form ye by twos,
Squads, or battalions, form as ye choose·
One is enough if he'll do what he can.
The glory of life is the dying for man!

IN MEMORIAM.

[Chicago, November 11th, 1887.]

Rare, gentle souls, tuned like a silver bell
    When struck by loving hand or kindly word,
    Yet keen and swift as Azrael's flaming sword

When menaced by the legal spawn of hell,
On whose foul shoulders Satan's mantle fell
    When legal might instead of free accord
    Was in the State set up to be adored,
Whose favors legislators buy and sell.
Thou didst not humble nor deny the right
    When press and pulpit yelled like dogs accurst,
But calmly looking in the face of Might,
    Didst bid the dastard crew to do their worst,
Smiling in sorrow, gentleness and grace
Upon the superstition of thy race.

ILLINOIS.

When the " Press, "—God save the mark—wishes to mould " public opinion " it is not very choice either in language or sentiment, Here is a sample which appeared on the eve of the execution of four of earth's grandest martyrs.
                                     —*The Author.*

" Let the sentence be swift, unerring and unmodified. Would it not be better to construct a huge dried beef cutter, and taking the least guilty one, go through him by very thin slices, applying a little brine between each slice. Let the most guilty ones look on, and be put through one by one until Parsons has seen Spies put through and his turn comes at last. Of course the slicing should be done from feet upward."— *Chicago Inter-Ocean.*

    State ! the proudest of the West,
    Martyr's blood is on thy crest ;
    Thou should'st know its value best.

When thy faithful Lovejoy fell,
Was not Slavery's dying yell
Born beneath the passing bell?

And less brave than them are we?
No more blood for liberty?
Pen, Press, Voice, and Men yet free?

In this drunken city's bed,
Thou by coward helots led,
Strike our trusty watchmen dead.

Dead, by murd'rous hangman's hand,
Dead, at princely thieves command,
Whilst aghast the people stand.

Hear the despot's shouts of glee,
" Firmer stands our thrones for thee ;"
" Law—not Justice for the free !"

Illinois, thy gory deed
Shall confront thee in thy need,
When thy very heart shall bleed.

When 'neath flames thy city lay,
Was there one to say thee nay,
When for money thou didst pray?

Begged'st thou then from door to door,—
And the lean hands of the poor
Freely swept thine ashen floor

Now, when women, children steep,
In their tears thy dainty feet,
Findst thou no mercy in thy keep ?

Harlot ! thou shall sue again,
Sue with tears of blood, in vain,
When shall break yon cloud of flame.

Hear ! While distant Peoples mourn,
Reck not thou the hovering storm,
That shall blight thy treach'rous form.

Freemen's hands that capped thy brow,
Freemen's hands assail thee now,
Freemen's hands shall smite thee low.

*　　*　　*

Lay our heroes gently down,
Crowning each with martyr's crown,
Heeding not of curse or frown.

Not a sigh we waste for them,
Not a tear their graves to gem,—
Theirs' a brighter diadem.

Throned in hearts now brooding woe,
In each hut that grief can show,
These—their monarchs—only know.

Each hour now's with danger fraught,—
For these huts and hearts well taught, ˊ
Bring all tyrant schemes to naught.

Taught, though scaffolds, rope and rod
Fell at law's death-dealing nod—
Taught *Humanity is God!*

———

TO ONE WHO WAS AFRAID TO SPEAK HIS MIND ON A GREAT QUESTION.

Shame upon thee craven spirit
   Is it manly, just, or brave,
If a truth have shown within thee,
   To conceal the light it gave ;
Captive of the world's opinion—
   Free to speak, but yet a slave ?

All conviction should be valiant ;
   Tell thy truth, if truth there be ;
Never seek to stem its current ;
   Thought, like rivers, find the sea ;
It will fit the widening circle
   Of Eternal Verity.

Speak thy thought, if thou beleiv'st it,
   Let it jostle whom it may,
E'en although the foolish scorn it,
   Or the obstinate gainsay ;

Every seed that grows to-morrow
Lies beneath the sod to-day.

If our sires, the noble hearted,
    Pioneers of things to come,
Had like thee, been weak and timid,
    Traitors to themselves and dumb,
Where would be our present knowledge
    Where the hoped millenium ?

Where would be triumphant Science,
    Searching with her fearless eyes,
Through the infinite creation
    For the soul that under lies—
Soul of beauty, soul of goodness,
    Wisdom of the earth and skies?

Where would be our great inventions,
    Each from by-gone fancies born,
Issued first in doubt and darkness,
    Launched 'mid apathy and scorn?
How could noontide ever light us,
    But for the dawning of the morn ?

Where would be our free opinion,
    Where the right to speak at all,
If our sires, like thee, mistrustful
    Had been deaf to duties call,
And concealed the thoughts within them,
    Lying down for fear to fall ?

Though an honest thought, outspoken,
   Lead thee into chains or death—
What is life, compared to virtue?
   Shall thou not survive thy breath?
Hark! the future age invites thee!
   Listen! trembler, what it saith!

It demands thy thought in justice,
   Debt, not tribute, of the free;
Have not ages long departed,
   Groan'd, and toil'd, and bled for thee?
If the past have lent thee wisdom,
   Pay it to Futurity.

———

OUR MARTYRS.

Under the cruel tree,
Planted by tyranny,
Crown in barbarity,
   Fostered by wrong;
With stately, soldier pace,
With simple, manly grace,
Each hero took his place,
   Steady and strong.

Wearing their robes of white,
As saints or martyrs might,
Calmly, in conscious right,
   Faced they the world.

While on each face upturned,
Sternly their sad eyes burned
Reproach, for blame unearned,
    Hatred had hurled.

Hatred, dull-eared and blind,
Hatred, of unsound mind,
Hatred, which gropes to find
    That which is worst.
How could it judge a heart,
Where wrong and suffering start
The throbbing valves apart,
    E'en till they burst?

How could it hear the call,
Through life's grim silence fall,
Sounding to waken all
    Those souls who sleep?
How could it see the height,
That to to those eyes was bright
Where, as a sun, in might
    Freedom shall sweep?

Not for the hearts that bled,
Not for the bride unwed,
Children and wives unfed,
    Should our tears be shed ;
But for the palsied brains,
But for the stagnant veins,
For the greed that sucks its gains
    From human woe.

One with a gentle word,
One with a sob unheard
Of warning love ; a third
    With triumph cry.
Meeting the rope's embrace,
Of gallows' old disgrace,
Making a holy place ;
    Thus did they die.

And when in later days,
Bards all sing lofty lays,
In Freedom's maker's praise
    Their names shall live ;
And hearts which cannot sing,
Shall the pure incense swing
Of love that all may bring
    That each will give."

                    —Anon.

    *   *   *   *

O poet child of light,
Soul-pure and sparkling bright,
White-winged as angel's flight
    Sweep'st thou the chord :
Down deep in human hearts,
From eyes the anguish starts,
From conscience with'ring smart
    Smote by thy word.

Let not my voice be stilled,
Let not my pen be willed,
Let not my soul be thrilled
　　　With less lofty strain ;
Till lust and greed apace,
All vanquished in disgrace,
Hunted from place to place
　　　Mocked in disdain.

Let all the earth rejoice !
Poets have yet a voice !
Honor hath yet a choice !
　　　Life yet a soul !
Courage hath yet a word !
Thunder it till all have heard !
Hasten with one accord !
　　　Freedom's the goal !

　　　　　　　　　　—*G. P. M.*

THE POET.

His home is in the heights : to him
Men wage a battle weird and dim,
Life is a mission stern as fate,
And Song a dread apostolate.
The toils of prophecy are his,
To hail the coming centuries—
To ease the steps and lift the load
Of souls that falter on the road.

The perilous music that he hears
Falls from the vortice of the spheres.
He presses on before the race,
And sings out of a silent place.
Like faint notes of a forest bird
On heights afar that voice is heard ;
And the dim path he breaks to-day.
Will some time be a trodden way.
But when the race comes toiling on
That voice of wonder will be gone—
Be heard on higher peaks afar,
Moved upward with the morning star.

O men of earth, that wandering voice
Still goes the upward way : rejoice !

THE INVOCATION.

An extract from the "Decoration Day Poem"
entitled Once a Year. Published by request
in the Emporia (Kas.) *Daily Democrat*, 3d
June, 1889.

O, Nature all beautiful—All bountiful God!
We praise Thee, we bless Thee, that under the sod
   The seed of its kind grows the richest flower,
   For having been kept awhile by the power
Of thine own reproduction, by the warmth of the sun;

By the dew-distilled vapor, and by every one
  Of thy manifold secrets of light, earth and sea,
  And man! the arbiter of his own destiny—
  "The measure and judge of the things that be"
Goes down to the grave—that part of the whole
Grand plan of progression where body and soul
  Commingle, unite, reproduced in perfection,
  Attended by the law of immutable resurrection,
And the last grand era shall heave up the sea
Of the slumbering ages, awakened and free !

————

AGITATE !

TABLE OF FIRST LINES.

THE PESSIMIST.

" I have gathered a posie of other men's flowers, and
nothing but the thread that binds them is my own."
—*Montaigue.*

"Again and again 'tis repeated,
From morn till the close of day,
(And the cities traffic and rattle)
And of sun's line there is scarcely a ray,"
—*Mrs. M. M. Lyle.*

"Mine be a cot beside the hill:
A bee hive's hum shall soothe my ear,
A willing brook that turns a mill
With many a fall, shall linger near."
—*Samuel Rogers.*

"Never so old as when we dream of youth
And long for it—a thing apart and gone."
—*Veley.*

"Touch us gently, Time !
We've not proud nor soaring wings;
Our ambition, our content
Lies in simple things."—*Crowell.*

"Would'st thou the unseen spirit see?
First begin to know thy self, and He
Will then be shadowed forth in thee."
—*Russian.*

"Hate the evil and love the good, and establish
justice in the gate." "Let justice roll down as waters,
and righteousness as a mighty stream."—*Hebrew
Prophecy*.

"Blow, blow ye winds with heavier gust!
And freeze, thou bitter biting frost!
Descend, ye chilly smothering snows,
Not all your rage, as now united, shows
More hard unkindness, unrelenting,
Vengeful malice unrepenting,
Than heaven-illuminated man to man on brother
    man bestow."—*Burns*.

All the rivers run into the sea,
O, thou bounding, brimming river,
Hurrying heart! I seem
To know (as one knows in a dream)
That in the waiting heart of God forever
Thou too shalt find the sea."
                    —*Elizabeth Stewart Phelps*.

"Art sick? art sad? art angry with the world !
Do all friends fail thee ?   Why, then, give thyself
Unto the forests and the ambrosial fields :
Commerce with them and the eternal sky.
Despair not, fellow.   He who casts himself
On Nature's fair, full bosom and draws food,
Drinks from a fountain that is never dry.
The poet haunts these.   Youth that never grows old
Dwells with her and her bowers : and beauty sleeps

In her most green recesses, to be found
By all who seek her truly."—*Barry Cornwall.*

Well said, well written, and well sung;
But "Merssrs. ten per cent" have wrung
The hope, the life, the very soul
From man, and Nature's bountiful.—*G. P. M.*

"What! not going to the country?"
—*Society Notes.*

"It is because the few have got control of all the
avenues of wealth, of all the channels of profit, and
appropriated the proceeds of the labors of the many.
They fence in every fountain, and bestride every
stream and dole out the waters grudgingly, in small
quantities, and for such service as they themselves
shall command."—*David Overmyer, in the Voice of
Labor, 1889.*

" Yes we may all congratulate ourselves that this
cruel war is nearing a close. It has cost a vast amount
of treasure and blood. The best blood of the flower of
American youth has been freely offered upon our
country's altar that the nation might live. It has
indeed been a trying hour for the republic ; but I see
in the near future a crisis arising that unnerves me and
causes me to tremble for the safety of my country. As
a result of the war, corporations have been enthroned,
and an era of corruption in high places will follow, and
the money power will endeavor to prolong its reign

by working upon the prejudices of the people until all wealth is aggregated in few hands and the republic is destroyed. I feel at this moment more anxiety for the safety of my country than ever before even in the midst of war. God grant that my suspicion may prove groundless.—*Extract from private letter : Abraham Lincoln.*

Were his fears groundless ? Read the following carefully, ponder over it with the plan laid down in the *' Hazzard Circulars,'* forget not that there were College Presidents, Professors of High schools, Teachers, Poets, Artists, Artisans and Laborers, 3,000,000 of them, tramping and begging for bread in 1873, that now, as I write, this cold, raw day Jan. 20th, 1890—40,000 idle men are tramping the streets of Chicago, from lack of work, all the result of the following diabolical so-called "Laws."

Laws of Financial Death.

1.   The law putting two exceptions in the United States notes, (greenbacks) passed February 25. 1862.
2.   The national banking law, passed March 25. 1863.
3.   The law authorizing the contraction of the currency, passed March 6, 1868.
4.   The act to strengthen the public credit (so-called,) passed March 18, 1869.
5,   The act to fund the national debt, passed July 14, 1870.
6.   The act demonetizing silver, passed March 12, 1873.
7.   The resumption act, passed January 14, 1864, to be consummated January 1, 1879.

**

Legislation that is bought, can no more be law than can varioloid be called small pox—symptoms are not disease.—*G. P. M.*

GREENBACKS?   Yes !

"Congress shall have power to declare war . . . . to coin money . . . . to regulate the value thereof."
—*The Constitution.*

"To coin—to make money ; to coin as a word."—*Worcester.*

When the war cloud had assumed formidable proportions.   Money was tendered to the government by Wall Street Brokers, "At from 24 to 36 per cent interest."—*Appleton' s Cyclopedia, for 1861, Page 296.*

"July 17, 1861, and February 12, 1862, came the "Enactments" authorizing the issue of $66,000,000 treasury notes, not bearing interest and payable for all debts, public and private.   These first issues of greenbacks constituted the demand notes, which, unlike all subsequent issues, did *not contain the exception clause*, consequently they have always been at par with gold.   Wherever gold went these demand notes could go, even into the coffers of the bondholders.   They paid his interest, paid duties on imports, the million-aire took off his hat to them, and the banks made obeisance."—*Emery.*

THE PROOF OF A CONSPIRACY

BETWEEN THE AMERICAN AND EUROPEAN BANKERS TO ROB THE PUBLIC.

Read this carefully. Ponder it well, and then make up your mind regarding you duty to vote for the party of the people.

CONSOLIDATED ROBBERS' ASSOCIATION, ESTABLISHED IN 1862.

HAZZARD CIRCULAR.

Slavery is likely to be abolished by the war power, and chattel slavery be destroyed. This I and my European friends are in favor of, for slavery is but the owning of labor, and carries with it the care for the laborer, while the European plan, led on by England, is capital control of labor by controlling wages. This can be done by controlling the money.

The great debt that capital will see to it is made out of the war, must be used as the means to control the volume of money. To accomplish this, the bonds must be used as a banking basis.

We are now waiting to get the Secretary of the Treasury to make the recommendation to Congress. It will not do to allow the greenback, as it is called, to circulate as money for any length of time, for we cannot control that, but we can control the bonds, and through them the bank issue.

THE BANK CIRCULAR.

DEAR SIR: It is advisable to "do all in your power to sustain such daily and prominent weekly newspapers, especially the agricultural and religious press, as will oppose the issuing of greenback paper money, and that you also withhold patronage or favors from all who will not oppose the government issue of money. Let the government issue the coin and the banks issue the paper money of the country, for then we can better protect each other. To repeal the law creating national bank notes, or to restore to circulation the government issues of money will be to provide the people with money, and will, therefore, seriously affect your individual profit as bankers and leaders. See your member of Congress at once, and engage him to support our interest that we may control legislation.

Immediately after the passage of the Legal Tender Act above cited, a bankers' convention assembled in Washington. The result of their "consultation" was the "exception clause" on the greenback, and was consummated February 25, 1862, "wherein it was stipulated that the greenback should be legal tender for all debts, public and private, *except duties on imports and interest on the public debt, which from that time forward should be paid in coin.*"

THE VOICE OF HISTORY.

The [legal tender] bill was no sooner made public than delegations of bankers from New York, Boston and Philadelphia hurried to Washington to oppose it. They organized in a formal manner by selecting a chairman (S. A. Mercer, of Philadelphia,) and invited the finance committee of the senate and the committee of ways and means of the house to meet them at the office of the Secretary of the Treasury, January 11, 1862. The invitation was accepted. At the meeting which followed the bankers spoke in opposition to the bill. * * * The bank delegates remained in Washington and held further consultations with Secretary Chase, extending through several days, which resulted in an arrangement with him to the effect, amongst other things, that congress should be urged to pass the National Bank bill, etc.—*Berkey's Monetary System, 1876.*

TESTIMONY OF THADDEUS STEVENS.

Mr. SPEAKER—I have a very few words to say. I
approach the subject with more depression of spirits
than I ever approached any question. No personal
motive influences me. I hope not, at least. I have a
melancholy foreboding that we are about to cosummate
a cunningly devised scheme, which will carry great
injury and great loss to all classes of people throughout this union, except one. With my colleague, I believe that no act of legislation was ever hailed with as
much delight throughout the length and breadth of
this union, by every class of people without exception,
as the bill which we passed and sent to the senate.
Congratulations from all classes, merchants, traders,
manufacturers, mechanics and laborers, poured in upon
us from all quarters. The Boards of Trade from Boston, New York, Philadelphia, Cincinnati, Louisville,
St, Louis, Chicago and Milwaukee approved its pro-
vision and urged its passage as it was.

I have a dispatch from the Chamber of Commerce,
Cincinnati, sent to the Treasurer, and by him to me,
urging the speedy passage of the bill as it passed the
house.

It is true there was a doleful sound came up from
the caverns of bullion brokers and from the saloons of
the associated banks. Their cashiers and agents were
soon on the ground, and persuaded the senate with
but little deliberation, to mangle and destroy what it
had cost the house months to digest, consider and pass.
They fell upon the bill in hot haste, and so disfigured

and deformed it, that its father would not know it. Instead of being a beneficent and invigorating measure, it is positively mischievous. It has all the bad qualities which its enemies charged on the original bill and none of its benefits. It now creates money, and by its very terms declares it a depreciated currency. It makes two classes of money, one for banks and brokers, and another for the people. It discriminates between the rights of different classes of creditors, allowing the capitalists to demand gold, and compelling the ordinary lender of money on individual security to receive notes which the government had purposely discredited. * * * All classes of people shall take these legal tender notes at par for every article of trade or contract, unless they have money enough to buy United States bonds, and then they shall be paid in gold. Who is that favored class? The banks and brokers and nobody else.—*Speech in house, February* 20, 1886.

TESTIMONY OF WM. D. KELLEY.

I remember the grand old commoner, Thaddeus Stevens, with his hat in his hand and his cane under his arm, when he returned to the house after his final conference (on the exception clause,) and shedding bitter tears over the result. "Yes," said he, we had to yield , the senate was stubborn. We did not yield until we found that the country must be lost or the banks gratified, and we have sought to save the country in spite of the cupidity of its wealthiest citizens."— *Judge W. D. Kelley, Philadelphia, January 15, 1867.*

Testimony of Henry Wilson.

It is a contest between the broker, jobbers and money changers on the one side, and the people of the United States on the other. I venture to express the opinion that ninety-nine of every hundred of the loyal people of the United States are for this legal tender clause.—*Wilson's Speech in the Senate, Feb. 15, 1882.*

"Next on the calendar" comes the National Banking Law, passed March 25, 1863.

Moulton's History of American Finances, page 131, states the case as follows :

Mr. Sherman now introduced the National Bank bill. After a lengthy debate it passed the Senate by a vote of 23 to 21. In the mean time there had been several bills for the same purpose introduced and referred to the committee in the house. When the senate bill come down it was not referred, as usual, but brought before the house without consideration in committee with other similar bills. It was not discussed in committee of the whole, but under a motion to refer, which cut off all amendments, the friends of the bill debated its general merits. When, by parliamentary tactics, it was forced to a final vote it passed under the gag rule of the previous question by a vote of 78 to 64.

"My agency in procuring the passage of the national bank act, was the greatest financial mistake of my life. It has built up a monopoly that affects every interest in the country. It should be repealed. But before this can be accomplished, the people will be arrayed on one side and the banks on the other, in a contest such as we have never seen in this country.'' —*Salmon P. Chase.*

''The two first steps of the plot as laid down in the ''Hazard Circular'' were now taken, viz: Abolition of chattel slavery, and the establishment of a bankers' currency, based on the public debt; a debt which was forced upon the people and for which there was no earthly use, but which was intended to be, and is, a curse.'' . . . .

The next step was to get rid of the greenback and *treasury note.* To accomplish this the ever-obedient Congress passed a law authorizing the Secretary (Mc-Culloch) of the Treasury to sell 5-20 bonds and with the proceeds *retire United States currency*, INCLUDING GREENBACKS. The Secretary was so anxious to do the bidding of the money-masters in the matter of pushing the contraction of the currency and the destruction of the greenbacks that the far-seeing Buffalo banker, E. G. Spaulding, a member of Congress, seeing a financial crash impending, wrote him as follows:

'' You no doubt, now, to a certain extent *have control of the currency of the country*, and I think that you will, of necessity, *contract moderately* (i. e., destroy more slowly), so as to preserve a *tolerably easy money market.* There may be *occasional spasms of tightness* for money, but generally I shall look for plenty of money for at least *a year to come.*''

"Did anybody ever read a more diabolical letter?"
—*D. P. Hubbard.*

This "Act" of Congress became "The Law authorizing the contraction of the currency," and passed March 6, 1866.

The other vicious "Acts" following each other in rapid succession were respectively :

The act to strengthen the public credit (so called), passed March 18, 1869.

The act to fund the national debt, passed July 14, 1870.

The act to "demon"-e-tize silver, passed March 12, 1873.

The resumption act, passed January 14, 1864, to be consummated January 1, 1879.

Thus was the "Hazzard Circular" literally carried out to the letter.

And what was all this done for ?

To make gold, alone, money.—*G. P. M.*

*   *   *   *   *   *

The machinery is now furnished by which in any emergency the financial corporations of the east can act together at a single day's notice with such power that no act of congress can overcome or resist their decision.—*New York Tribune in 1874.*

" We are now one in Commercial interests with England. The Bankers of America,—3000 of them,—the monopolist and speculator rule America by controlling the money of the country, and they also con-

trol the vast army of Labor by having this mighty
engine of power in their lawless hands. Ruin stares
us in the face ! Shall we tamely submit ? or, shall
we loyally rebel ? is the question of the hour."—*D. P.
Hubbard.*

" No people in a great emergency ever found a faithful ally in gold. It is the most cowardly and treacherous of all metals. It makes no treaty it does not
break. It has no friend it does not sooner or later
betray, armies and navies are not maintained by gold.
In times of panic and calamity, shipwreck and dis-
aster, it becomes the agent and minister of ruin. No
nation ever fought a great war by the aid of gold. On
the contrary, in the crisis of the greatest peril, it becomes an enemy more potent than the foe in the field ;
but when the battle is won and peace has been secured,
gold reappears and claims the fruits of victory. In
our own civil war it is doubtful if the gold of New
York and London did not work us greater injury than
the powder and lead and iron of the rebels. It was the
most invincible enemy of the public credit. Gold paid
no soldier or sailor. It refused the national obligations.
It was worth most when our fortunes were the lowest.
Every defeat gave it increased value. It was in open
alliance with our enemies the world over, and all its
energies were evoked for our destruction. But as
usual, when danger has been averted, and the victory
secured, gold swaggers to the front and asserts the supremacy.—*Ingalls' speech in the U. S. Senate, February* 15, 1878.

ALMOST A TRAGEDY.

" Do you ask for an apology ?"—*Dean.*

" This is my apology."—*Westphal.*

" Honest men are rarely rich."—*Booth.*

" Homeless a vagabond he wanders the earth."-—
Old Song.

> " Out in the cold world, out in the street,
>   Asking a penny from each one I meet."
> —*Post War Song.*

" Meantime, the tramp, tramp, tramp, sounds on,—
the tramp of sixty thousand yearly victims. Some
are besotted and stupid, some are wild with hilarity,
and dance along the dusty way, some reel along in
pitiful weakness, some wreak their mad and murderous impulses on the helpless women and children whose
destinies are united with theirs, some go bound in
chains from which they seek in vain to wrench their
bleeding wrists, and all are poisoned in body and soul,
and all are doomed to death.—*J. G. Holland.*

" Abolish want and you abolish crime."—*Treat.*

" Prudence indeed, will dictate, that governments
long established should not be changed for light and
transient causes ; and accordingly all experience hath
shown that mankind are more disposed to suffer while

evils are sufferable, than to right themselves by abolishing the forms to which they are accustomed.   But
when a long train of abuses and usurpations, pursuing
invariably the same object, evinces a design to reduce
them under absolute despotism, it is their right, it
their duty, to throw off such government, and to
provide new guards for their future security."—*Declaration of Independence.*

Viewed in the light of *Looking Backward.*   How
prophetical are the words of the following extract :
" And, sir, where American liberty raised its first voice,
and where its youth was nurtured and sustained, there
it still lives, in the strength of its manhood, and full
of its original spirit.   If discord and disunion shall
wound it—if party strife and blind ambition shall
hawk at and tear it ; if folly and madness, if uneasi-
ness under salutary and necessary restraint, shall succeed to separate it from that Union by which alone its
existence is made sure, it will *stand, in the end, by
the side of that cradle in which its infancy it was rocked;*
AND IT WILL FALL AT LAST, IF FALL IT MUST, amid
the proudest monuments of its own glory, AND ON
THE VERY SPOT OF ITS ORIGIN."—*Webster.*

" And now, sirs, to my apology."—*Kempis.*

"Serfdom and aristocracy are, in fact, the correla-
tives of each other.   Wherever there are serfs, then
there are autocrats; and wherever there are are autocrats, there, then, are serfs; and though the laborers

of England are not serfs in one sense, inasmuch as they may emigrate if they can find the means, they are to all intents and purposes serfs so long as they remain in England.   It is a mere fallacy to suppose that serfdom has been abolished in England.   It has not been abolished; it has only been generalized.   .   . Serfdom, or even slavery, may be abolished in appearance, and yet retained in reality, *the means of compulsion being changed* with the advance of society, which would no longer tolerate the open employment of individual force."—*Dove*.

"The ownership of land is the basis of autocracy. .   .   .   The simple privilege of the ownership of the soil produced, on the one side the lord, on the other the vassal—the one having all the rights, the other none.   The right of the lord of the soil acknowledged and maintained, those who lived upon it could only do so upon his terms.   .   .   .   The English land owner of to day has, in the law which recognizes his exclusive right to the land, essentially all the power which his predecessor, the feudal baron, had.   .   .   .   Between the condition of the rack rented Irish peasant and the Russian serf, the advantage was in many things on the side of the serf."—*George*.

' Let the political arrangements be what they may, let there be universal or any other suffrage, so long as the aristocracy have all the land, and derive the rent of it, the laborer is only a serf, and a serf he will remain until he has uprooted the rights of private landed property.   The land is for the nation, and not for the aristocracy.   We affirm, then, that serfdom has not been abolished, but only generalized, in England, Ireland and Scotland.   .   . A serf is a man who, by the arrangements of mankind, is deprived of the object on which he might expend his labor, or of the natural profit that results from the labor, and conse- quently, is under the necessity of supporting himself and his family by his labor alone.   And a lord, or an autocrat, is a man who, by the arrangements of man- kind, is made to possess the object, and who, conse- quently, can support himself and his family without labor, on the profits created by the labor of others.''— *Dove, page 153.*

"And what is *the cause* of human pauperism and degredation ?   For the two go hand in hand. , . . . Does any man suppose that the nation will much longer believe that Britain cannot support its inhabitants? Does any man believe that the men who can make steam engines, cotton mills, and railroads, and ships, and the largest commerce in the world, and spinning jennies, and steam printing machines, and Skerryvore lighthouses and electric telegraphs, and a thousand other wonders, could not make such a distribution of Britain as should enable every man in it, and many more, to earn an abundant livelihood by their labor? Does any man believe this?   And if he does not be- lieve it, does he suppose that any superstitious notions about the king's right to grant the soil to individuals will long stand in the way *of their doing it?*   If En- glishmen discover that pauperism and wretchedness are *unnecessary;* that the degradation of the laboring population, their *moral* degradation consequent on poverty, is the curse of *the laws* and not of nature— does any man suppose that Englishmen would not be Justified in abolishing such laws, or that they will not abolish them ?   Can we believe for a moment that if any arrangements would enable the population to find plenty, that such an arrangement will not be made ? If any man believe this, he is at all events willing to be credulous.   For ourselves we believe it not "— *Dove, page* 312.

" Place one hundred men on an island from which there is no escape, and whether you make one of these men the absolute owner of the other ninety-nine—or the absolute owner of the soil of the island, will make no difference either to him or to them.

In the one case, as in the other, the one will be the absolute master of the ninety-nine—his power extending even to life and death, for simply to refuse them permission to live upon the island would be to force them into the sea.

Upon a larger scale, and through more complex relations, the same cause must operate in the same way and to the same end—the ultimate result, the enslavement of laborers, becoming apparent just as the pressure increases which compels them to live ou and from land which is treated as the exclusive property of others.

Take a country in which the soil is divided among a number of proprietors, instead of being in the hands of one, and in which, as in modern production, the capitalist has been specialized from the laborer, and manufactures and exchange, and all their many branches, have been separated from agriculture. Though less direct and obvious, the relations between the owner of the soil and the laborers will, with increase of population and the improvements of the arts, tend to the same absolute mastery on the one hand, and the same abject helplessness on the other, as in the case of the island we have supposed. Rent will advance, while wages will fall. Of the aggregate produce, the landowner will get a constantly increasing, the laborer a constantly diminishing, share. Just as removal to cheaper land becomes difficult and impossible, laborers, no matter what they produce, will be reduced to a bare living, and the free competition among them, where land is monopolized, will force them to a condition which, though they may be mocked with the titles and insignia of freedom, will be virtually that of slavery,"—*Progress and Poverty, page* 250.

"Was it for this that the Almighty made man in his own image and gave him the earth for an inheritance? Was it for this that he sent his Son into the world to proclaim the divine benevolence, to preach the doctrine of human brotherhood, and to lay the foundation of a kingdom that should endure forever and ever? We do not believe it, neither do we believe that pauperism comes from God. It is man's doing, and man's doing alone. God has abundantly supplied man with all the requisite means of support; and

where he cannot find support, we must look, not to
the arrangement of the Almighty, but to the arrangements of men, and to the mode in which they have
portioned out the earth.   To charge the poverty of
man to God, is to blaspheme the Creator instead of
bowing in reverent thankfulness for the profusion of
his goodness.   He has given enough, abundance, more
than sufficient ; and if man has not enough, we must
look to the mode in which God's gifts have been dis-
tributed.   There is enough, enough for all, abundantly enough ; and all that is requisite is freedom to labor
on the soil, and to extract from it the produce that
God intended for man's support."—*Dove, page 308.*

"All can know that in a land so capable of yielding
a bountiful harvest, into the willing hands of labor as
is America, that when want arises, it must come
through some outside cause, wrong, and unnecessary."
—*G. P. M.*

"Friends : I come not here to talk. Ye know too well
The story of our thralldom ; We are slaves !
The bright sun rises to its course, and lights
A race of slaves ! He sets, and his last beam
Falls on a slave !"—*M. R. Mitford.*

  "And shall I never have a home
   O say ! my fellows, say !
  Is there no room for such as me
   In all America."?—*Ingraham.*

THE MUSTER—A PROPHECY.

"THE EARTH HATH HE GIVEN TO THE CHILDREN OF MEN."—*Bible*.

"THE LAND HAVE I GIVEN FOR AN HERITAGE TO ALL PEOPLE."—*Bible*.

"THE LAND SHALL NOT BE SOLD FOREVER, FOR THE LAND IS MINE."—*Bible*.

"MOREOVER, THE PROFIT OF THE EARTH IS FOR ALL."—*Bible*.

"WOE UNTO HIM THAT USETH HIS NEIGHBOR'S SERVICE WITHOUT WAGES AND GIVETH HIM NAUGHT FOR HIS WORK."—*Bible*.

"The original robbers of the people's land, not satisfied with having ground enormous rents out of the sweat of the toilers all these years, propose to perpetuate this dishonest villainy forever. * * * For a small part of the State of Pennsylvania, perishable blankets were given in exchange for imperishable land. * * * * That is the only semi-honest *original* title to land. All the rest has been stolen by the right of might and murder. The sword was used to write the title deeds instead of the pen, and blood is used instead of ink, and death was dealt out instead of money. And this is the foundation that so-called sacred vested rights stand on.

They say that although my title was originally bad,

a hundred years has made it good.   But I say that no
length of time can ever convert an original robbery
into an honest transaction, and justice can never sleep
so long that she has no right to wake and reform."—
Looking Forward.

***

" A change of society is as much to the interest of
those who have property as it is to those who have
not, and if they **are** not fools they will help us change
the coming revolution into a peaceful evolution.   But
Carlisle said that England was a nation of twenty-six
millions inhabitants, mostly fools.   If that is true of
America, we may have a revolution."—*Prof. Orchardson.*

" Then woe to the rule that has plundered,
    And trod down the wounded and slain,
While the wars of the old time have thundered.
    And men poured their life tide in vain ;
The day of its triumph is ending,
    The evening draws near with its doom,
And the star of its strength is descending,
    To sleep in dishonor and gloom."—*Jas. G. Clark.*

Thousands have been led to ask :
"How comes it that, notwithstanding man's vast
achievements, his wonderful efforts of mechanical in-
genuity, and the amazing productions of his skill, his
own condition in a social capacity should not have
improved in the same ratio as the improvement of his

condition with regard to the material world? In Britain man has to a great extent beaten the material world. He has vanquished it, overpowered it; he can make it serve him; he can use not merely his muscles, but the very powers of nature, to effect his purposes; his reason has triumphed over matter; and matters, tendencies and powers are to a great extent subject to his will. And, notwithstanding this, a large portion of the population is reduced to pauperism, to that fearful state of dependence in which man finds himself a blot on the universe of God—a wretch thrown up by the waves of time, without a use and without an end, homeless in the presence of the firmament, and helpless in the face of the creation. . . . . . Is it a matter of necessity that there shall be paupers (that vile word) in the richest country in the world? Is it true that England can no longer support Englishmen; nor Ireland, Irishmen; nor Scotland, Scotchmen? Have we, in fact, arrived at the last term of population, and must all, over and above, expatriate or starve? Is this true, or is it false? . . . . . Either pauperism and degradation are the work of the Creator of our system, the All Powerful who has placed present man in circumstances where the natural capabilities of the earth are insufficint for his support; or pauperism and degradation are the work of fallen man, who, through ignorance, has based his arrangements of the earth on superstitious propositions, and thereby necessarily has rendered it impossible that the amount of good intended by the Creator can be extracted from the earth. . . . . . . The evil is expressed in a few words;

and sooner or later, the nation will appreciate it and
rectify it. It is 'the alienation of the soil from the
State, and the consequent taxation of the industry of
the country,' Britain may go on producing with
wonderful energy, and accomplish far more than she
has yet accomplished. She may struggle as Britain
only can struggle. She may present to the world
peace at home when the nations of Europe are filled
with insurrection.

She may lead foremost in the march of civilization
and be first among the kingdoms of the earth. All
this she may do, and more. But as certain as Britain
continues her present social arrangement, so certainly
will there come a time when—the other questions
being cleared on this side and on that side, and the
main question being brought into the arena—the labor
of Britain will emancipate itself from thraldom. Grad-
ually and surely has the separation been taking place
between the privileged land owner and the unprivi-
leged laborer. And the time will come at last that
there should be but two parties looking each other in
the face, and knowing that the destruction of one is
an event of necessary occurrence. That event must
come. . . . Of the two parties, one must give way.
One must sink to rise no more ; one must disappear
from the earth. The continued existence is incom-
patible. Nature cannot support both. And when
once this last great question of liberty has been disposed of, the country cannot fail to commence another
evolution, and enter on a line of progress that shall
ultimately place men on the equality with regard to

natural property that will then prevail with regard to political liberty."—*The Theory of Human Progression.*

"The great social problem, (for the whole world) then, ... is, "TO DISCOVER SUCH A SYSTEM AS SHALL SECURE TO EVERY MAN HIS EXACT SHARE OF THE NATURAL ADVANTAGES WHICH THE CREATOR HAS PROVIDED FOR THE RACE; WHILE, AT THE SAME TIME, HE HAS FULL OPPORTUNITY, WITHOUT LET OR HINDRANCE, TO EXERCISE HIS SKILL, INDUSTRY, AND PERSEVERANCE FOR HIS OWN ADVANTAGE."—*The Twentieth Century.*

No truth can be more absolutely certain, as the intuitive proposition of the reason, than that "an object is the property of its Creator," and we maintain that creation is the only means by which an individual right to property can be generated.

Consequently, as no individual and no generation is the creator of the substantive, earth, it belongs equally to all the existing inhabitants; that is, no individual has a special claim to more than another. But while on the one hand we take into consideration the object—that is, the earth—we must also take into consideration the subject; that is, man and man's labor.

The object is the common property of all, no individual being able to exhibit a title to any particular portion of it.

And individual or private property is the increased value produced by individual labor. But the perma-

nent earth can never be private property—although
the laws may call it so, and may treat it as such—it
must be possessed by the successive generations that
succeed each other on the face of the globe? . . . .
How can the division of the advantages of the natural
earth be effected ?   By the division of its annual value
or rent ; that is, by making the rent of the soil the
common property of the nation.   That is, (as the
TAXATION is the common property of the state), BY
TAKING THE WHOLE OF THE TAXES OUT OF THE
RENTS OF THE SOIL, AND THEREBY ABOLISHING ALL
OTHER KINDS OF TAXATION WHATEVER."—*P. E.
Dove.*

Then "Take the land it is thine own."—*The
Muster.*

———

AMERICA.

———

AN ADDRESS TO THE AMERICAN " HOUSE OF LORDS "
IN BEHALF OF THE " COMMONS."

———

" A HUNDRED MEN WITH A MILLION A YEAR,"
" A MILLION MEN WITH A HUNDRED A YEAR."

***

" This could not be if justice reigned."

***

"The gulf is widening between Dives and Lazarus at a geometrical ratio, and if this impracticable society could possibly run fifty years longer, there would be ten men with a hundred million a year and twenty million with nothing.   But it cannot last half that time, for when millions of willing workers are hungry in the presence of legally stolen wealth, their respect for the law evaporates."—*Looking Forward.*

**

"Any thing that a man can make it is his as against all the world.   Anything that a man cannot make, that exists independent of him, such as air, water and land is a gift of bountiful nature to all her children.   Tyrants would *corner* the air if they could." —*Prof. C. Orchardson.*

"Civilization is impossible when material success is dependent on the development of the evil that is within us"   .   .   .   .

"The private enterprise system of preventing the production of wealth, patch it or modify it as you may, it is so short-sighted and vicious to the core that it can never do anything but spread poverty and woe broadcast"   .   .   .   .

"The weapons of the past were sword and shield. The adepts in the use of those openly robbed the workers of their wealth.   The weapons of the present are lobbying bills, purchasing legislatures, first and second mortgage bonds, preferred stocks, common stocks, speculation, adulteration, cornering markets and ownership of machinery."—*Prof. Orchardson.*

"The United States Senate is a pampered set of bloated obstructionists who obtain their seats by bribery and fraud and delegate their duties to irresponsible sub-committees whose business it is to deceive themselves."—*McIntyre.*

"The spawn of most fish sinks, but that of the pike and shark rises to the surface of the water."—*Science.*

"Show me the law of the country and I will show you the condition of the people."—*The Earl of Chatham.*

"THE EXCEPTION CLAUSE," consumated by Act of Congress, February 25, 1862. This is the "act" that crippled the greenback, making it read "Except Duties on Imports and Interest on the Public Debt." It is needless to say that this "*base act*" was *not* "obstructed" by the United States Senate ; but was hurried to President Grant, who, it is said, "signed it without even looking at it"—no wonder that the monumental scheme at Riverside is an elephant on the hands of the committee ; for a poet has said—"Grant said that he did not know the nature of this bill, But his negligence was devilish and decidedly criminal." —*G. P. M.*

The National Bank Act, passed in 1863. Of all the villainous schemes of robbery ever practiced upon

any people, our national bank system stands pre-emi-
nent.   This also was ratified and perpetuated by the
"American House of Lords," of whom the poet has
written :

"The leaders to that fearful strife
For sordid gain, are leaders still ;
Who wield the whip that smites the life
In freedom's name, from vale and hill.
                                —*G. P. M.*

"THE CONTRACTION ACT," April 12, 1866, was
passed, whereby it was provided that a regular and
systematic cremation of greenbacks should take place.
Let it be remembered that upon this government
money, the greenback, the people did not pay interest.
It was backed by the government, which made it safe
and reliable, and issued in sums convenient for small
as well as large business transactions.

"THE CREDIT-STRENGTHENING ACT," March 18,
1869.   It is claimed by many bond holders and their
leaders, that the act which authorized the issue of
Bonds to which this act refers, made them payable in
gold.   But there is no such possible interpretation of
the act, else, why this very act? Grant, Sherman
and Morton were parties to this soulless act.

"THE REFUNDING ACT," July 14, 1870, provided
for the refunding of the national debt. In other
words, it was a scheme to perpetuate the debt, and a
plot against the people to keep them forever under the
yoke of bondage

THE DEMONETIZATION OF SILVER ACT, passed in 1873, was only another name for Contraction, another scheme to rob the people.   It was not the American capitalist alone who entered into this murderous plot for demonetization of silver.   In the Banker's Maga-zine of August, 1873, we find the following on the subject :

In 1872, silver being demonetized in France, Eng-land and Holland, a capital of $500,000 was raised, and Earnest Seyd, of London, was sent to this country with this fund, as agent for the foreign bond holders and capitalists, to effect the same object (demonetiza-tion of silver), which was accomplished.   There you have it, a paid agent of English capitalists sent to this country with $500,000 to buy the American Congress and rob the American people.   In corroboration of this testimony we read from the *Congressional Record* of April 9, 1872, page 2,032, these words :

Earnest Seyd, of London, a distinguished writer and bullionist, who is now here, has given great atten-tion to the subject of mint coinage.   After having ex-amined the first draft of this bill (for the demonitiza-tion of silver) he made various sensible suggestions, which the committee adopted and embodied in the bill.

''THE RESUMPTION ACT, January 24, 1875, author-ized the secretary of the treasury to destroy the frac-tional currency, and issue silver coin in like denomi-nations to take its place.   The people had found the fractional currency convenient, not only as a medium of exchange at home but especially cheap and conve-

nient for small remittance in trade.   The destruction
of this money was a serious injury to the business
men of the country, for without fractional currency,
even small remittances incurred the expense of a draft
or money order.   But Congress appeared to be looking after the interests of the money-monger, and not
the prosperity of the country, so it next became necessary to issue bonds with which to purchase the silver
bullion authorized for coinage.   Let it be remembered
that these were untaxed, interest-bearing bonds, and
of such large denominations that only capitalists were
able to carry them, while to the debt-ridden people
was added the interest of these very bonds, which
could only exist by the destruction of the greenbacks
and fractional currency upon which the public paid
no interest.''—*Emery*.

If a man should borrow $50 and give his note for
$100, and then, after paying interest for twenty-five
years beg for the privilege of paying $125 for the note,
would you call that able financiering?   Yet that is
exactly what Uncle Sam has been and is doing—buy-
ing bonds at $125—$125 paid for $100, for which he
received $50.   Who gets the difference?   The mon-
eyed man who stayed at home to speculate while the
boys went to war and saved the country.   Who pays
the difference?   The men who work, for labor pays
everything.   And yet many soldiers who got 50 cents
on the dollar while in the field, to support their families at home, now vote with the ''grand old party,''
because they continually pat him on the back and

point to the South and stir up the old enmity. The
soldier is made to forget his own interest, and take up
and howl for the interest of Capital, which controls the
old party leaders. Fact, every word of it. And if
you will only open your eyes and look the matter
squarely in the face, you can't help seeing it.—*Indus-
trial Appeal.*

ABOLISH IT.

" The election of United Staters Senators by popular
vote would make a nice twin to ballot reform."—*K.
C. Times.*

It would certainly be an improvement on the present system of selling the positions to the highest bid-
der, but why not abolish the relic of feudalism and
despotism entirely. The Senate was copied from the
House of Lords of England, to represent the property
and the gentry of America and to hold the common
people in check, and it has served the purpose admir-
ably. But the common people think they are now
sufficiently civilized to govern themselves, and that
the gentry and property of America seem to fare very
well indeed, even in the House of Representatives.
A bill has been introduced in the English House of
Commons to abolish the House of Lords, and why
should the republic retain the copy longer than a
monarchy retains the original ? Is America going to
let England so far out-strip her in the progress
towards freedom and true Democracy ?"— *The (Topeka
Kan.) Jeffersonian.*

" Rev. C. M. Sheldon, pastor of the Central Congregational Church of this city, is preaching a series of able sermons on social problems. Wishing to ascertain for himself if work could be had in Topeka by those needing it, he disguised himself in a rough suit of laborer's clothes and after a day spent in applying at every place where work was likely to be found he discovered no opportunity of earning his supper.'

***

"On the same night that Mrs. Martin, of New York City, gave a ball which cost her fifty thousand dollars, another woman, a refined and educated married woman of thirty, with a sick and helpless husband, committed suicide because she had tramped the streets through the storm and without food until utterly exhausted in search of honest work. The letter she left to her sick husband was very pathetic and told how she could only find subsistence by combining wifely duties with domestic service for widowers or bachelors."—*The Jeffersonian, January 23d, 1889.*

A Pregnant Prophecy.

"The republic west of us will have its trial period, its darkest of all hours. It is traveling the high road to that direful day. And this scourge will not come amid famine's horrid stride ; nor will it come by ordinary primitive judgments. It will come as a hiatus in statescraft a murder-bungle in policy. It will be when health is intact, crops abundant, and the munificent hand open. Then so-called statesmen will cry 'overproduction;' the self-reliant, self-potent, will go to the ballot-box amid hunger and destitution, (but surrounded with the glitter of self-rule) and ratify by his ballot the monstrous falsehood, 'overproduction' uttered by mis-statesmen, and vindicate by the same ballot, the infamous lie ; 'overproduction,' thrown upon the breeze by a senile editor, through a corrupt press.   And this brings ruin upon his country, serf_dom upon himself and death or oppression upon his children."—*Thomas Carlyle.*

WHY FARMERS ARE POOR.

Farmers are not usually aware of the great interest earning values of city, suburban, and mining lands, forests and other valuable real estate, nor do they realize that the enormous income derived by the owners of these valuable properties, are to a great extent a burden on the farmer.

Nothing has interest earning value, nor can have, without power to tax production.

All wealth is produced by labor, and all incomes of wealthy men consist of rent, interest and profits, paid by labor, either directly or indirectly.   Much of what is called profits is really interest, and nearly all interest, when analyzed. will be found really rent.

The total annual value, or income earning power, of the real estate alone, not counting buildings and other improvements, but only the bare land, of the four cities of New York, Chicago, Kansas City and St. Louis, is fully one thousand millions of dollars.   This vast sum is a tax on production, and is paid by small tolls on every dollars' worth of produce seeking a market, and by every dollars' worth of goods sold, manu- factured, or shipped through these cities.   As farmers are the great producers and consumers of goods they must of course pay the greatest amount of these tolls, which eventually find their lodgment in the pockets of the real estate owners.   The charges of stockyards, grain elevators, commission men, and all classes of merchants and manufacturers must be sufficient to pay, first, the salaries of employes; second, interests on buildings, machinery, stock, and other active capi- tal; third, rent of—or interest—on the value of real estate occupied ; and fourth, profits, taxes and insur- ance.   In the four cities above named, and in all other large business centers, rent or interest on value of land exclusive of all improvements, is found by ac- tual careful investigation to equal or exceed all other charges and expenses.   The largest incomes in Amer- ica are those of the Astors, the Goelets and other real estate owners of New York City.   Potter Palmer, who owns nothing but Chicago real estate, has the most palatial residence west of the Alleghenies, and of over forty millionaires in Kansas City and over seventy in St. Louis, every one has made their money in the rise of real estate, and have nearly all their money invested in real estate.

The terminal facilities of railroads, and their yards, shops, depot grounds, etc., in towns and cities passed through aggregates a land value of more than half the total value of the roads and equipments, hence half of all net profits of railroads goes to pay rent.

Mines of coal, lead, iron, zinc, copper and other metals, and pine or other forest lands, are almost exclusively the property of wealthy men and corporations, and draw from farmers and other production enormous rents. At least a hundred millionaires are known to derive their incomes from coal and other mines, and Michigan alone has ten men worth from five to fifty millions each, whose only property is pine lands. California's two hundred millionaires are all land owners and indebted to use of land values for their wealth.

Land values are determined by their location. The fact that land is used for farming or stock raising is of itself evidence that it has no location value, but only a use or labor value, and under a just system of taxation should pay little or no tax. If land has a location value it cannot and will not be profitably used for farming, but will be put to the more valuable use required by its location.

From the above analysis it will be seen that farmers are now the great rent-payers to millionaires and corporations, as well as the great tax-payers for the entire nation. It is estimated by the best statisticians that more than three-fourths of the total national tariff and revenue taxation is paid by farmers. This would amount to three hundred millions annually, and as the tariff and revenue taxes are known to put five dollars in the pocket of monopolies for each dollar of real tax it makes a burden of one billion eight hundred million dollars per year on farmers, in addition to all state, county and local taxation, of which they pay the bulk.

It will be seen that all values are diffused through all production and consumption, and that all incomes consist of tolls levied upon producers through rents, interest, profits and taxes."—*W. H. T. Wakefield.*

EMBALM IT.

"FAREWELL! A LONG FAREWELL TO ALL MY GREATNESS."—*Shakspeare.*

"AND NOW THE MARTYR IS MOVING IN TRIUMPHAL MARCH, MIGHTIER THAN WHEN ALIVE."—*H. W. Beecher.*

"John Maynard," with an anxious voice,
 The captain cries once more,
"Stand by the wheel five minutes yet
 And we will reach the shore."
                    —*Anonymous.*

" Down ! down !" cried Mar, "your lances down !
Bear back both friend and foe."—*Walter Scott.*

" Make way for liberty !" he cried,
Then ran with arms extended wide,
As if his dearest friend to clasp ;
Ten spears he swept within his grasp.

"Make way for liberty !" he cried ;
Their keen points crossed from side to side ;
He bowed among them like a tree,
And thus made way for liberty.
—*James Montgomery*.

Ring the alarum bell :—Murder and treason
Banquo, and Donabain ! Malcolm ! awake !
Shake off this downy sleep, death's counterfeit,
And look on death itself !—Up, up, and see
The great doom's image !—Malcolm ! Banquo !
As from your graves rise up, and walk like spriets,
To countenance this honor !
O Banquo ! Banquo !—*Shakspeare*.

CONCERNING FLAGS.

A subscriber asks us to define just what is meant by
the red flag of anarchists and socialists? Now, this
asking us to define things had better be stopped before
it makes us trouble—or a liar. We never saw but one
red flag, and that we helped capture from a band of
border ruffians, in Kansas, in 1856, and even that was
not all red, for it had a white half moon in one corner.
There is nothing more nonsensical or more of a hum-
bug than the flag business. Unless a flag symbolizes
an idea and represents a living principle of value to the
human race it is indeed "nothing but a pole with a rag
on it." And the worst of it is, the same flag may really
symbolize the most sacred rights and aspirattons of
humanity in one generation and the most oppressive

plutocracy or despotism in the next, or the reverse may be true. The British flag in America in 1776 represented despotism and an attempt to stamp out the liberties of the American colonies, yet the British flag to-day waves over the freest people on earth, even if they do have the meaningless figurehead of royalty left. What patriotic young American of thirty or more years ago has not felt his pulses thrill as he gazed on the Star Spangled Banner and thought of Lexington, Bunker Hill and Yorktown, and of the heroic struggle of his forefathers to make this "The Land of the Free and the Home of the Brave?" And yet the same flag to-day waves over a great many things that no American is proud of, including a presidency bought "in blocks of five" or at wholesale, with fat fried out of protected monopolies. It waves over a senate of millionaire plutocrats whose seats were bought in the open market; over Gould, Vanderbilt and Huntington's railroads and telegraph lines which charge all the traffic will bear and traffic in legislatures as in stocks or cattle. It waves over a land of which one-third in value is held by foreign nobles and syndicates, who draw a yearly revenue of seven hundred million dollars from the toil of American laborers—a land which contains more tenant farmers by one-third than does the three kingdoms of England, Scotland and Ireland. The Star Spangled Banner now symbolizes a government that enters the homes of the poorest widows and sewing girls and takes a large part of their scanty earnings in taxes on their thread, needles, oil, tea, sugar, salt, clothing, blankets, coal; etc., taxing them one-half

their scanty savings, even though the widows little
ones go hungry and the girl is driven to the
street to escape starvation, while the millionaire
is taxed but one per cent of his savings, and is allowed
the use of militia and sheriffs' posses free of cost to
make his "hands" stand another reduction of wages.
Perhaps these things are all right (from a modern
standpoint), but we. hardly think it was intended by the
men that carried the flag at Ticonderoga and Valley
Forge, and we doubt if any young American's heart
swells with pride and rapture as he sees it wave over
a squad of militia shooting at striking coal miners
whose wages would not keep the coal mine owner's
valet in cigars, while the miners' wives are feeding
their little ones on boiled weeds and the refuse of slop
barrels.

We spent five years, one month and two days during
the late unpleasantness—the best years of our young
manhood—in service under the stars and stripes, that
it might wave over a free people and united country,
but somehow things don't seem to have turned out just
as we expected them to, and the lash of necessity seems
to crack as loud and sting as sharply as the lash of the
overseer formerly did.

But really, we are not answering our correspondent's question about red flags, and guess we scarcely
know how to do so.

Red flags are used in Spanish bull fights, to make
the fool bull rush on the cold steel that is to pierce his
spinal marrow, and national flags are used to make
the workingmen become food to the powder of other

workingmen with whom they have no quarrel. Were there no national flags there could be no rich men's wars and poor men's fights. When some big thief wants to steal a whole state he yells out: "Our flag is insulted!" and straightway thousands of men on each side begin shooting and stabbing each other, although there is no reason on earth why they should not be the best of friends, except that each side has a pole with a rag tied to it to "defend."

But, about that red flag, we can only give second hand information, and that our correspondent could have gotten without putting us to all this trouble. A writer of acknowledged authority says: "The red color of our flag signifies that all nations and all mankind are one blood. It symbolizes the common fatherhood of God and Brotherhood of Man, hence is the flag of peace and fraternity, and once it is universally adopted wars will become impossible, for no man will fire on his own flag—the flag of all Humanity, the flag of peace and universal brotherhood."

All this sounds very pretty and Christ-like, but such a flag will never be popular with generals, commissaries, quartermasters, colonels, majors, captains, chaplains, shoddy contractors, "statesmen" politicians, thieves, bummers, pirates, gamblers, speculators, etc., and these are the fellows that run things. No, the red flag might do very well in Heaven but its no good for this practical earth.—*W. H. T. Wakefield, in The Topeka Jeffersonian.*

"Is it any wonder that the world is an intellectual poor-house when it is the policy of all the so-called leaders of the human race both in religion and secular thought, to kill every new idea before it is fairly born ? Happily truth cannot be suppressed, otherwise our present rulers, including majorities, would run the world back to animalism by breeding in and in. . . . . We are taught with our drawing consciousness that patriotism is one of the noble instincts of the mind. We are taught that we should love America and Americans better than any other land or people. Ah, yes. If it were not for that cry : "For God and Native Land" how would despots and plutocrats maintain their sway. It is to the interest of kings that the people of different nations should hate each other. It is to the interest of manufacturers that workmen of different lands should look upon each other as competing rivals. Patriotism—one of the meanest emotions of which man is capable—what is it but the repression of love between men which if patriotism could be broken down would make of the world one people. Cosmopolitanism is better than patriotism. . . . How can the world be rich in love as long as men love a flag better than they love a fellow ; as long as they arm themselves to fight against each other ; as long as they separate themselves by title and genealogical tables and bank account ?"—*Hugh O. Pentecost, in October Twentieth Century.*

AGITATE !

THE TREE OF STATE.

"The people are the roots of the State ; if the roots are flourishing the State will endure."—*Chinese Maxim.*

"The relations of structure are actually such, that, by the help of a central regulative system, each organ is supplied with blood in proportion to the work it does."—*Herbert Spencer.*

"So distribution should undo excess
And each man have enough."—*King Lear.*

"Is not a dollar a day enough to buy bread ? Water costs nothing, and a man who cannot live on bread and water is not fit to live."—*H. W. Beecher.*

"The time is near when they (the banks) will feel themselves compelled to act strongly ; meanwhile a very good thing has been done ; the machinery is now furnished by which, in any emergency, the financial corporations of the east can act together at a single day's notice with such power that no congress can overcome or resist their decision."—*The New York Tribune.*

Speaking of capitalists, Lawrence Gronlund says : "*These are the offspring of the 'Let Alone' policy.*"— *Laissez-faire.*

"Let alone"—leave the upright at the mercy of the cunning ; leave the ignorant to teach themselves ;

leave every one who profits by a corrupt system to make the most for himself; let labor remain something wholesale out of which fortunes are made and which during that process yields such and such a percentage of Misery and Sin—what a grand "principle!" By adopting it for its guiding-star our society has achieved—*Anarchy.*

Here is the proof: "The strongest of this generation wants a dictator. I say come on with your schemes of confiscation and forced loans and graduated income tax and irredeemable currency, under universal suffrage, and if you are sufficiently frank in proclaiming the doctrines of your ringleaders, then under military necessity and even here in the United States we must get rid of universal suffrage, and we shall. Rather than allow these things we will have one of the fircest of civil wars."—*The Rev. Joseph Cook.*

"We need a strong government; the wealth of the country demands it. Without capital and capitalists our government would not be worth a fig. The capital of the country demands protection. Its rights are as sacred as the rights of the paupers who are continually prating of the encroachments of capital and against centralization. . . . . The wealth of the country has to bear the burden of government, and it should control it, there will be no political change of administration. . . . To avert fearful bloodshed a strong central government should be established as soon as possible."—*The Organ of the Late Senator Sharon, the Nevada Chronicle.*

The New York *Herald*, "with a frankness and sagacity quite commendable, said : "Our people please themselves with the fancy that they are free, because they have the right to meddle a little with politics now and then, in conventions, in legislature and similar places; they chatter and twaddle and scream like so many crows and jays over the eternal principles of freedom as secured in the political fabric. Meanwhile the great economical facts of life, the facts that are and always were the really shaping and controlling forces in the political destinies of a people sweep rapidly and certainly forward, on lines that indicate the will and movement of a despotic spirit. *In that movement a great collision with the popular will is in preparation.*"

"Behold! Now I, too, have my twenty thousandth part of a Talker in our National Palaver. What a notion of Liberty !"—*Carlyle.*

"The Spartans made money of iron. Congress has exercised nearly the same prerogative. The gold value of the nickel five cent piece is exactly four-sevenths of one cent; and the government has made a profit to this date of four million six hundred and eighteen thousand dollars by this coinage. I have heard these pieces called "tokens." They are "tokens," just as the silver dollar or *double eagle* are "tokens," They are convertible into any other lawful money. A nickel worth four-sevenths of one cent will purchase five cents worth of any commodity just as certainly and cheaply as five cents worth of gold, because the nation has so decreed. The same is true of our subsidiary silver coinage, which has been alloyed to such an extent that the country is nearly six million dollars richer by the seigniorage."—*Extract from a Speech Delivered in the U. S. Senate, February 15, 1878, by John J. Ingalls of Kansas.*

In a speech recently delivered in Topeka the Hon. David Overmyer said :

"It would require a volume to detail the long list of outrages committed against these defendants (the Anarchists) by this Judge (Gary) upon the so-called trial. His monstrous mocking of everything righteous, just and lawful ; his total, open and conscious disregard of law stands without a parallel in American history. Incredible as it may appear, it is now very generally believed that the jurors were paid a very large sum each for the conviction of these men by the citizens of Chicago.

On August 20, 1877, the following appeared in the Chicago *Tribune* over the signature of one E. A. Mulford. "The long agony is over, law has triumphed. Anarchy is defeated. The conspirators have been promptly convicted, let them be as promptly punished. The twelve good men and true, whose honesty and fearlessness made a conviction possible should not be forgotten. They have performed their unpleasant duty without flinching. Let them be generously remembered—raise a fund, say $100,000, to be presented with the thanks of a grateful people. A

certain N. B. Ream, also proposed to head the list
with $500.

'Judge Gary, in discharging the jury, said, among
other things.' "It does not become me to say any
thing in regard to the case you have tried, or the verdict you have rendered, but as men compulsorily serv-
ing as jurors, as you have done, you deserve some
recognition of the services you have performed, besides the meagre compensation you are to receive.
You are discharged from further attendance upon this
court. I understand that some carriages are in attendance to convey you from this place." "Ah,
indeed ; here we have it. Capital ready to pay for the
verdict, and the judge who sat at the trial fully aware
of the fact." "Impossible as it may appear, this out-
rage upon human rights, this mockery of justice, was
sustained and upheld by the Supreme court of Illinois
in an opinion that will stand, while it does stand, as a
monument of judicial falsehood, corruption, degradation and despotism, a source of humiliation and sorrow to every true lawyer, and a solemn warning to the
people to put no man upon the bench who is not in
sympathy with them in their never-ending struggle
with power. The supreme court of the United States
having held that it had no jurisdiction in the case,
and General Butler before that court having pronounced the Chicago trial anarchy itself, on the 11th
of November, 1887, the four remained under sentence
of death were judicially assassinated and deliberately
murdered under the form of law. The horrible deed
cast a gloom over the working people of the whole

land and of the whole world.   To millions of hearts it
brought doubt as to man's attainment to better conditions.   To thousands it brought despair, and to
thousands of others a feeling that it was their solemn
duty to resist to any extremity the further prostitution
of the law in the name of the law.   .   .   .   .   I refer
to these matters to show you that as matters stand,
your proposed agitation for a reduction of the hours of
labor may find itself limited by the lawless interference of those in authority.   What has happened in
the past may happen again, if you will permit it.   If
you desire to better the condition of people by agitation, the first step is to assure yourself that you will
not be denied the right to agitate ; to secure beyond
a peradventure the uninterrupted exercise of your constitutional right of peaceful assemblage, free speech
and free press ; yea, free as the winds of heaven, for
less than that is not freedom.   This you cannot expect
while public opinion condemns to life imprisonment
men whose only offence was that they contended for
better conditions for the people.   The same public
opinion which condemns them will condemn you if the
necessities of organized capital require it.   While they
remain in prison you will remain in chains.   Whether
you agree with their views or not, your cause is their
cause and their cause is your cause.   They are not imprisoned for crime ; they are imprisoned for opinion's
sake—for having dared to assail the capitalistic pluto-
cratic despotism which now holds this whole country
in its grasp, and which will never release its grasp
until compelled to do so.

Until a public sentiment is formed sufficiently potent to open wide the iron door of the Joliet prison and bid Schwab, Fielden and Neebe go free, you need not expect but little improvement in your condition, because the fundamental condition of improvement will be wanting, viz, : a feeling of absolute freedom to say what you please respecting questions of capital and labor. When that happy day shall come ; when the accursed conspiracy laws shall be swept away ; when organized bands of lawless murderers shall no longer be tolerated ; when the cities are relieved of the despotism of a state appointed police, and permitted to exercise the great American right of local self-government ; when the people shall have learned that the state and the law are merely an agency and not a guardianship, much less a fetish to be worshipped ; when public opinion will no longer endure privileged classes and persons ; when every man mayfreely vote and speak as he pleases concerning any matter or man, without the fear that his views will be construed into sedition, treason and murder, then, and not till then, may we look forward with bright anticipations to that golden age which seers have described and prophets have foretold."—*Hon. David Overmyer.*

AGITATE!

THE GROOMING OF THE GIANT.

" MOREOVER, THE PROFIT OF THE EARTH IS FOR ALL."—*Bible*.

" Woe unto him that useth his neighbor's service without wages, and giveth him nought for his work.—*Bible*.

" Be careful, sirs ! how you judge God's revolutions as the product of man's invention."—*Oliver Cromwell*.

"The Revolution is the work of the Unknown. Call it good or bad, as you yearn toward the Future or the Past."—*Victor Hugo*.

" Will not one French Revolution suffice, or must there be two? There will be two if needed ; there will be twenty if needed ; there wiil be just as many as needed. "—*Carlyle*.

"It is not to die, or even to die of hunger that makes a man wretched ; many men have died ; all men must die.   But it is to live miserable we know not why ; to work sore and yet gain nothing ; to be heart-worn, weary, yet isolated, unrelated, girt in with a cold universal *Laissez-faire*."—*Carlyle*.

" We all can see that there are all over our country energies which can find no employment, or, at all events, minds which are cruelly compressed into duties far too narrow, and, on the other hand, work which remains undone for want of adequate energies, because no systematic attempt has yet been made to estimate the real needs of the social organism and to distribute its forces in accordance with them.—There is no organic adjustment anywhere."—*The " Value of Life."*

" Man has it in his power by his voluntary actions to aid the intentions of Providence, but to learn these intentions he must consider what tends to promote the general good."—*J. S. Mill.*

" Mankind, without any common bond, any unity of aim, bent upon happiness, has sought each and all to tread their own paths, little heeding if they trample upon the bodies of their ' brothers' in name, enemies in fact. This is the state of things we are in to-day." —*Mazzini.*

" Competition gluts our markets, enables the rich to take advantage of the necessities of the poor, makes each man snatch the bread out of his neighbor's mouth, converts a nation of heathen into a mass of hostile, isolated units, and finally involves capitalists and la- borers in one common ruin."—*Gregg.*

"The citizens of a large nation, industrially organ- ized, have reached their possible ideal of happiness, when the producing, distributing and other activities are such that each citizen finds in them a place for all energies and aptitudes, while he obtains the means of satisfying all his desires."—*Herbert Spencer*.

"In 1860 the agricultural population of the United States were two-thirds owners and one-third tenants of the land. In 1880 they were one-third owners and two-thirds tenants. In twenty years one-third of the tillers of the soil had been disinherited and turned out of their possessions to become tenants of the land they once owned, or join the mighty and daily augmenting army of wage laborers, who throng all the avenues of life and struggle with each other in a fierce competition for employment."—*Hon. David Overmyer*.

On the 14th of February, 1879, in the United States Senate, John J. Ingalls said: "We cannot disguise the truth that we are on the verge of an impending revolution. Old issues are dead. The people are arraying themselves on one side or the other of a portentous contest. On one side capital, formidably entrenched in privilege, arrogant from continual triumph, conservative, tenacous of old theories, demanding new concessions, enriched by domestic levy and foreign commerce, and struggling to adjust all values to its standard. On the other side is labor, asking for employment, striving to develop domestic industries, battling with the forces of nature and subduing the wilderness. Labor starving and sullen in the cities, resolutely determined to overthrow a system under which the rich are growing richer and the poor poorer, a system which gives to a Vanderbilt wealth beyond the dreams of avarice, and condemns the poor to a poverty which has no refuge from starvation but the grave. Our demands for justice have been met with indifference and disdain; the laborers of the country asking for employment are treated like impudent mendicants begging for bread."

"No labor agitator, nay, not even the condemned anarchists, ever arraigned capitalistic despotism in stronger terms than did Mr. Ingalls. All that he said was then true, and it is all true now, with the horrors which he described increased in a ten-fold ratio, and with the alternative not far ahead of a prompt return to reason and right or the bloodiest revolution recorded in history. And, yet, the senator is strangely silent upon this subject. The same power which holds labor bound hand and foot has entirely silenced this once bold and potent advocate of the people's cause. Dire distress and gaunt starvation now stalk through the land like the wierd precursor of desolation. The eye, that ten years ago, could see the cause of their coming is now blind to their presence. The voice that could then proclaim the approaching danger, now awed into silence, is heard no more. What wonder, then, that those who labor for the men who wield this mighty power are obliged to call upon others than their employers to redress their grievances, right their wrongs and mete out justice to them? What wonder that they must make their humble appeal to the public at large to grant them through law, a slight reduction of their hours of toil?"—*Hon. David Overmyer.*

"Most of the Americans remember the rising of the workingmen in July, 1877. That rising was to all Socialists, also to those who held aloof from it, a most promising sign. The first revolt of American white slaves against their task-master. That it was accompanied by excesses by the most neglected stratum of society was unfortunate but unavoidable. This stratum is just the worst heritage which capitalism leaves on our hands. In a very short time we shall have another series of years of "hard times." . . . . We expect another revolt then, more serious than the first. That most likely will also be surpressed with comparative ease. A few more years elapse. Another "crisis," yet more severe, shows its hideous head. The screws of distress are turned yet more on the wage-workers. Another most serious revolt. Possibly powder and shot will suppress that, too.

But in the *fullness of time* we shall have a labor revolt that will not be put down. Then is the time for energetic Socialist minority to exert its influence. There is nothing that the people in such a crisis hail more than *leaders*, nothing they hunger and thirst more after than clear-cut, definite solutions. All the horrors of the French Revolution and the sad fact that Napoleon the I. became a necessity were due to the circumstances that the revolution had no leaders. We do not mean to say that that revolution was a failure, for it *did* accomplish every one of its objects: the abolition of privileges, the dispossession of the landowners and free competition, but the price paid was exorbitant. In our civil war, on the other hand, it was the abolitionists that successfully assumed the leadership, and probably exerted all the influence to which they were entitled.

That, the Socialist minority must do when *the* crisis comes, and make out of a revolt—another *revolution*.

Be confident the people will follow. In such times men become awake, shake off nightmares; the experience of years is crowded into hours. Novelties, which at sight inspire dread, become in a few days familiar, then endurable, then attractive."—*The Co-operative Commonwealth.*

" Nay, must we not rather confess, that that unlovely creature, the habitual office-seeker, is as natural a product of our political and social conditions as the scrub-oak is of the soil, when it has been laid waste by the removal of the primeval forest?"—*Richard Grant White, N. A. Review, July 1882.*

" I believe that party, instead of being a machinery necessary to the existence of free government, is its most dangerous foe, and that in order to get anything which really deserves the name of republican government, we must destroy party altogether.—*A True Republic, by Albert Stickney.*

" I think the time has come when the leaders of our political parties need to be taught that however important agencies these parties may be in the nation, they are only agencies. They are nothing more.

They are the servants, not the masters, of honest men.
The nation is our master, the right is our master.
God is our master, and conventions and parties are
only the instruments whereby we serve the nation for
the ends of right and truth.   If they prove fit instruments, we keep them in use.   If they fail us, we dis-
card them.   No matter how long and well they may
have served us—the servant is not above his lord—
and if a political party called into being to gain a
righteous end, and for a time fulfilling its mission
faithfully, then becomes a minister of unrighteousness,
its high achievements in the past, however glorious,
give it no more claim for employment in the future
than do the safe and speedy voyages which a ship has
made warrant us in sending it richly freighted again
upon a stormy sea when we find its timbers rotten and
itself no longer able to stand a storm."—*President See-
ley*.

"The most wealthy must govern in every state,
and will, regardless of any attempt to deprive them of
that right."—*Richmond (Va.) Whig*.

'"We need a strong central government ; the wealth
of the country has to bear the burdens of the government and shall control it."—*Senator Sharon*.

Aye! and this is the way they bear it.

REVENUE REEORM.

———

FRANK P. CRANDON, ILLINOIS STATE REVENUE COM-
MISSIONER, CHICAGO.

Section I of Article IX, of the Constitution of Illinois, declares :

*   *   *   *   *   *

" The General Assembly shall provide such revenues
as may be needful by levying a tax, by valuation, so
that every person and corporation shall pay a tax in
proportion to the value of his, her, or its property—
such value to be ascertained by some person or persons
to be elected or appointed in such manner as the General Assembly shall direct, and not otherwise."

*   *   *   *

Kinds of Property.	Valuation for Cook County.	Valuation for the State of Illinois.
Gold and silver plate and plated ware.	$ 14,815	$ 59,521
Diamonds and jewelry.	16,765	49,073
Franchises.	52,080	90.334
Moneys of bank, banker or broker.	654,350	2,853,362
Credits of bank, banker or broker	67,800	1,056,900
Bonds and stocks.	112,285	679,563

These items are selected as illustrative of all personal property assessments, and the figures suggest
all the comment that is required."—*The Statesman,
February, 1889.*

"It is astounding, yea startling, the extent to which the faith prevails in money circles in New York that we ought to have a king."—*New York Tribune, in 1874.*

> "If I could be as fly as a flea ;
>   With an auger like a mosquito,
> I'd tap the "Grant boom" just at the flume
>   And Hayes the Dictator with a veto.
>   —*G. P. M. in 1878.*

"We have arranged the programme for both parties, and are willing the people should exercise their choice of men."—*James Buell, Secretary National Bankers Ass'n.*

"It is the business of governments to protect the interests of business men, and they in turn will look out for the poor."—*President Garfield.*

"The only way we can control the working man is to make him eat up to-day what he earns to-morrow."—*Tom Scott.*

"He (the tramp) has no right but that which society may see fit of its grace to bestow upon him. He has no more rights than the sow that wallows in the gutter, or the lost dogs, that hover around the city square."—*Scribners Monthly.*

"It is time the Jeffersonian Declaration was laid on the shelf.—*W. W. Guthrie.*

"Hand grenades should be thrown among those who are striking to obtain higher wages, as, by such treatment they would be taught a lesson, and other strikers would take warning by their fate."—*Chicago Times.*

When the lion or the tiger or any other beast of prey ;
Shows his 'ivorys' as a warning of his instinct thus
    to slay—
Do his keepers fuss and pat him and coddle him to
    bed ;
Or do they take a red hot poker and punch his craven
    head???—*G. P. M.*

"The active cause of human development is found in the democratic spirit that prompts organized resistance to encroachments upon the natural rights and acquired privileges of the great body of the people. The counteracting force of tyranny by its usurpations compels defensive resistance, and finally aggressive warfare. The progress of the manual laborers who were slaves, then serfs, and are now termed freemen, is marked by the associated efforts of members of their class, and by the opposition of those antagonistic interests, the employers; the unemployed, the cultured, the comfortable, and those who govern or rule the political society called government. Whatever the motive of an association, the methods must partake largely of those of their antagonists.

Freemen combine, tyrants conspire. The combination of freemen to overthrow tyranny may be forced

to work secretly, but such secrecy is not a conspiracy ;
it is a confession of tyrannical power. The power of
discharge, which means banishment or starvation, may
be met with the freeman's power to strike, even to the
enforced bankruptcy of the antagonist. Those who
narrow their conception of a truth by adhering to the
literal dictionary definition of a word, and whose conception of the meaning of words and benefits of cus-
toms are founded upon past theories, confuse themselves and those with whom they have influence, when
they apply the word conspiracy to the associated efforts
of men who seek greater opportunities of life, liberty
and the pursuit of happiness."—*George E. McNeil, in
the December number of The Arena.*

AN ADVANCING CAUSE.

The successful termination of the London dockmen's
strike and a number of other minor struggles for an
increase of wages which have attracted less attention
than their importance demands, owing to the concen-
tration of public attention on the principal conflict, in-
dicates a wonderful advance in English public sentiment in relation to the labor question. It is about the
first important English strike in which public opinion
has ranged itself clearly and unmistakably on the side
of labor. Hitherto when any considerable number of
wage slaves revolted against the harsh and oppressive
conditions of their existence with the object of miti-
gating in ever so small a degree the evils of their lot,
the English press, representing the well-to-do and

conventionally respectable element, has, as a matter of
course, taken the part of capitalism.   In place of ex-
pressing sympathy with the toilers they have treated
them to hypocritical dissertations as to the exceeding
folly of strikes and the right of the capitalist to purchase his labor in the cheapest market.   It has been
the fashion to treat every sign of discontent among
workers as the result of the teachings of "agitators,"
and to assume that unless told of their wrongs by
outsiders such a thing as demanding an increase of
pay or a shortening of hours would never enter into
the heads of workingmen.   The influence of the church
as well as that of the press, has also with almost un-
varying uniformity been thrown into the scale against
labor struggling for its rights.   Strikers have been
exhorted to patience and submission here in the hope
that the joys of another world may prove a recom-
pense for their sufferings in this, and the sternest de-
nunciations of the pulpit have been directed, not
against oppression, but against those who ventured
to aid the oppressed.

The vast change which has come over English public sentiment within a very short period can be measured by the contrast between the position assumed by
the press and the pulpit of to-day in regard to the
dock-laborers' strike and their former treatment of
such movements.   No more phenomenal and radical
alteration in popular opinion could well bell be imag-
ined than that which has come about in the English
way of looking at social questions.   Almost the entire
press was loud in its expressions of sympathy with the .

strikers.   The customary platitudes about the right of
capitalism to do as it pleases with its own and the im-
possibility of increasing wages, inasmuch as the
" wages fund" was insufficient, were conspicuously
absent.   All which a strongly expressed and all but
unanimous expression of public sentiment in favor of
granting the modest demands of the strikes could do
to compel the surrender of the monopolies was done
by the newspaper press.   A still greater surprise if
possible was the favorable attitude of the various religious bodies.   The action taken by the venerable
Manning as a mediator between the parties, to which
is largely due the ultimate success of the movement,
and the active support of many religious organiza-
tions, whose efforts in providing food for the strikers
and their families prevented much suffering and probably many deaths, are signs of an awakening to the
wrong and injustice of the present social system, as
gratifying as unexpected.   The work of the social reformers who for generations have toiled, hoping against
hope, in the endeavor to arouse the masses to a determination to assert their rights, is at last bearing fruit.
The social revolution moves very slowly in conservative England, but it does move, and the patient incul-
cation of the great truth of the right of the worker to
the wealth he creates seems at last to have thoroughly
leavened public opinion.   One very powerful factor in
creating this remarkable change of feeling has certainly been the land agitation and the struggle for
Irish Home Rule.   The issue between a handful of
British and Irish landlords and the disinherited masses

of the people having got into politics, the broad question of the general social condition of the workers and the causes of their enslavement has been forced upon public attention.   In place of the discussion of empty, high-sounding abstractions and issues having no practical bearing upon the welfare of the people, the amelioration of the lot of the poor and the problem of the distribution of wealth have presented themselves as living, tangible questions.

It is never well to expect too great things in the way of a change of public feeling.   Doubtless there were special and local causes why the London press, usually so unfair and malignant in its treatment of labor matters, found itself ranged for the first time against a particularly obnoxious monopoly.   The reactionary forces may be expected to reassert themselves before long and prevent any such pronounced departure from the customary bourgeois habit of thought, as might be inferred, from the altogether exceptional action of the exponents of public opinion during the late critical period.   But making every allowance on this score, labor reformers have occasion for congratulation over the marked advance of our cause in Great Britain as evidenced by the influences which enabled the London dockmen to win their strike.''—*Journal United Labor, October 3, 1889.*

———

AGITATE!

THE LIGHT OF PERSIA.

"Faith builds a bridge across the gulf of death."
—Young.

"Heaven from all creatures hides the book of fate,
All but the page prescribed their present state."
—Pope.

" There are whole veins of diamonds in thine eyes,
Might furnish crowns for all the queens of earth.
—Bailey.

The soul's dark cottage, battered and decayed,
Lets in new light through chinks that *Time* has made."
— Waller.

" The light of the will hovering close to the sight ;
Is a most potent force when wielded for right."
—Joel.

" Yet *none* but *one* the scepter long did sway
Whose conquering name endures until *this* day."
— Wallace.

"Zeal and duty are not slow,
But on occasion's forelock watchful wait."
—Milton.

" To scatter plenty o'er a smiling land,
And read their history in a nation's eyes."
—Gray.

"Let our frail thoughts dally with false surmise."
—*Milton.*

" He conquers all with mildly beaming eyes."
—*Love.*

" I scarcely understand my own intent;
But silk-worn like, so long within have wrought,
That I am lost in my own web of thought."
—*Dryden.*

" There's a divinity that shapes our ends,
Rough hew them as we will."
—*Shakespeare.*

"'Tis with our judgments as our watches: none
Are just alike, yet each believes his own."
—*Pope.*

"One sally of a hero's soul,
Does all the military art control."
—*Dryden.*

" Whose game was empires, and whose stakes were
thrones,
Whose table earth, whose dice were human bones."
—*Byron.*

" He cast off his friends as a huntsman his pack,
For he knew when he wished he could whistle them
back."—*Goldsmith.*

" Sired of ye Sun and Air,
    Foal'd in ye angle of Might !
Caught in descent ; was ye glare
    Ye liquified Devil of light."—*Cibler*.

' And "Silence," like a poultice, comes
To heal the blows of sound."—*Holmes*.

I wake, emerging from a sea of dreams
Tumultuous, where my wreck'd, desponding thought
From wave to wave of fancied misery
At random drove, her helm of reason."—*Young*.

Self is the medium least refined of all,
    Through which opinion's searching beams can fall;
    And, pausing there, the clearest, steadiest ray
Will tinge its light, and turn its line astray."

—*Moore*.

" Let come what will, I mean to bear it out,
And either live with glorious victory,
Or die with fame, renowned for chivalry.
He is not worthy of the honey-comb,
That shuns the hive because the bees have stung."

—*Shakespeare*.

" It [*Vril*] can be stored in a small wand, which
rests in the palm, and, when skillfully wielded, can
rend rocks, remove any natural obstacles, scatter the
strongest fortress and make the weak a perfect match

for any combination of number, skill and discipline."
— *The Coming Race: Bulwer.*

" He stood, and measured the earth ; he beheld and drove asunder the nations ; and the everlasting mountains were scattered, the perpetual hills did bow ; His ways are everlasting."—*Bible.*

"What if this 'Vril' is but a poetic anticipation of the civilizing power of that real, energetic substance which we call—*dynamite !*"—*The Co-operative Commonwealth.*

"From hill to hill the mandate flew,
From lake to lake the tempest grew,
　　With waking swell,
Till proud oppression crouched for shame.
And Austria's haughtiness grew tame ;
And Freedom's watchward was the name
　　Of William Tell."—*Anonymous.*

"Think you that a drop of water, which to the vulgar eye is but a drop of water, loses everything to the eye of the physicist, who knows that its elements are held together by a force which, if suddenly liberated, would produce a flash of lightning?—*Herbert Spencer.*

" A laborer earning $1.00 a day—a good deal more than the average wage—that he works steadily along, that he never loses a day's work, that he is never sick,

that he lives like a Chinese, and thus is able to save
up half of his wages, $1.00 a day.   It will take him
more than 3,000—three thousand— years to accumu-
late a million !"—*The Co-operative Commonwealth, Lov-
ell's Library, Number 1,096.*

The Constitution reserves to itself the right of emi-
nent domain :   "No man is in law the absolute owner
of lands. . . . .   The State is thus fully entitled
to take charge of *all* instruments of Labor and Production, and to say that all social activities shall be
carried on in a perfectly different manner.   Undoubtedly the whole fleecing class will interpose their so-
called "vested rights."   That is to say because the
State for a long time tacitly allowed a certain class to
divide the common stock of social advantages among
themselves and appropriate it to their own individual
benefit, therefore the State is estopped, they say, from
ever recovering it.   And not alone will they claim un-
disturbed possession of what they have, but also the
right to use it in the future as they have in the past :
that is, they will claim a "vested right" to fleece the
masses to all eternity.

But such a protest will be just as vain as was that
of the Pope against the loss of his temporal sovereignty.   The theory of "vested rights" never applies
when a revolution has taken place ; when the whole
structure of society is changed.   The tail of a tadpole
that is developing into a frog may protest as much as
it pleases ; nature heeds it not.   And when the frog is

an accomplished fact, there is no tail to protest."—
The Co-operative Commonwealth.

THE GREAT READING STRIKE.

CONGRESSMEN INTERVIEWED ON THE SUBJECT.

Last week we mentioned that the New York *Herald*
had placed our American congressmen on record respecting the great Reading mine and railroad strike,
which had reduced to actual suffering a million of people, more or less ; and had brought discomfort, incon-
venience and loss to thirty millions more in the Northern States.

The published interviews of congressmen fill over
six columns of closely printed matter in the *Daily
Herald* of January 11. We have room for only a few
specimens. We quote from the *Herald* as follows :

Mr. Allen (rep.), of Michigan.—I believe in the
rights of organized labor as the only solution of the
labor problem. They have succeeded in righting
many wrongs, and laborers have the same right to
combine as the railroads.

Mr. Anderson (rep.), of Kansas.—As an abstract
proposition my opinion is that the men would not have
struck unless they had some imperative reason for it.
The corporation has the power to oppress them in many
ways, and will exercise it solely with a view to making money for the company, first in lower wages paid
to the men, and second in stock speculation, depressing the securities of the road for the purpose of un-

loading at high figures and purchasing at low figures. My sympathies are with the men.

Mr. Bayne (rep.), of Pennsylvania.—So far as I have been able to get at the facts of the case, they lead me to think the men are right in demanding higher wages.   I think they ought to be better paid.

Mr. Brumm (rep.), of Pennsylvania, is the Representative of the district in which the strike is on. His opinion is therefore given in full.   He said :   The men are undoubtedly in the right.   When the agreement with the miners expired, January 1, the price of coal was much higher than when the agreement was made. Notwithstanding this fact the Reading attempted to reduce the wages of its miners, and this reduction is what the miners are resisting.   In the region affected by the scale the $2.50 basis prevails, with an increase of 21 cents per ton for every three cents advance in the price of coal.   From what I have heard from reliable men I think the whole thing is a stock jobbing operation.   I have been credibly informed that many of the stock holders unloaded their stock when it had · reached a high figure.   This is evidence to me that they knew this trouble was coming.

The miners' strike, however, should not be confounded with that of the railroad men.   In the first instance I think the railroad men were wrong, and they so acknowledged it and returned to work.   But Sweigard, who is the chief bulldog of the oppression, repudiated his agreement and refused to re-instate some of the men.   In this, I think, the railroad company was wrong.   This whole thing is an attempt on the part of the Reading company to crush out organized labor. While I cannot prophesy as to the outcome, I have hopes that the men will be successful.

Mr. T. J. Campbell (dem.), of New York.—If the railway company has made an agreement with a body of honorable men, which I understand to be the case as between them and their employes, they should be compelled to carry it out.

Mr. Guenther (rep.) of Wisconsin.—As I understand it, the railroad company is trying to crush out the Knights of Labor. I do not think they have any right to make war on a labor organization at the expense of the public who have to buy coal.

Mr. Hall (dem.), of Pennsylvania.—In my own experience with somewhat similar employes, although we have sometimes disagreed, I have never found them unreasonable when they were fairly brought to see the facts in the case. I think if the railroad company would treat their men frankly and in a spirit which would show that they were not seeking to take unfair advantages, the strike would soon be settled. Yet I would not say there are not grievances on both sides. There usually are.

Mr. Hogg (dem.), of West Virginia.—My sympathies are with the laboring men, when they are right, as they usually are.

Mr. Landes (dem.), of Illinois.—I am satisfied the employes have not been properly compensated for their labor.

Mr. Hagan (dem.), of Louisiana.—The blame rests with the party denying the right to a conference. The workingmen are not paid sufficiently in proportion to the profits of their employers.

Mr. Laird (rep.), of Nebraska.—I would not attempt to speak off-hand of the merits of the dispute, but if congressional interference through the tariff has any terrors for our friends in Pennsylvania they had better look out. We may put the coal operators of Canada and Wales at work as a remedy for these frequent disturbances, which amount to public calamities to many communities. Why, as far away as Nebraska, I hear, although I hope it is not true, this fight has almost doubled the price of coal, and unless we can supply ourselves from Trinidad, Colorado, we are threatened with coal famine in midwinter. It is a terrible thing that thousands of people should hold their tenure of comfortable life at the mercy of the caprice or cupidity of any set of men. Such conditions invite desperate remedies. Why shouldn't we open our ports to anybody who has anything to burn that will protect our people against the recklessness or rapacity of such men? Or why should not the state or national government, as a last resort, condemn and reclaim their coal lands? They may make communists out of Congressmen if these outrages continue.

Mr. Lawler (dem.), of Illinois.—Workingmen do not throw themselves out of employment in midwinter except for good and sufficient reasons.

Mr. Lind (rep.), of Minnesota.—While I would not presume to give an opinion on such information as I have in the case, I will say that upon general principles my sympathies are with the strikers. I believe that in many cases the strikes are provoked by the coal barons, as we call them out west, that they may have a pretext for raising the price of coal.

Mr. Vance (dem.), of Connecticut.—It seems to me that when the price of coal is advancing, and the wages of the laborers are being decreased at the same time, the men have some justice on their side.

Mr. Weaver, of Iowa.—So large a body of men are not striking without good cause. They belong to an organization and are subject to a constitution which forbids them to strike without cause. I presume they have acted discreetly. The unjust aggregations of capitalists who form trusts and other combinations to the detriment of labor are the cause of most of these strikes. The combinations are so welded together that they are more powerful than the state, and, like the brigands of Italy, they have in their employ an army ot bravos, known among us as the Pinkerton detectives, and who are about as unnecessary as their Italian prototypes. The people will find a remedy for these things by and by. Meanwhile my sympathies are always with the laboring classes, for I believe they are wronged and oppressed at almost every turn of the government wheel.

Mr. White (rep.), of Indiana.—I think the men are right every time. If any humanity had been exhib-ited toward the men they would not act unreasonably or unruly. As a rule strikers proceed from the oppression of employers. The greed of corporations very generally impels their men to strike.

Mr. Whiting (rep.), of Massachusetts.—I believe the strike was caused because the company wanted to reduce wages eight per cent. As the company was doing a good business, such a movement, it would seem to me, was injudicious, as there was no necessity for it. The fact of the strike occurring at this particular season of the year, when there is the greatest demand for coal, would rather convey the suspicion that the company wanted to advance prices.

Mr. Yost (rep.), of Virginia.—Right and justice are apparently with the strikers.

Senator McPherson (dem.), of New Jersey.—I think the right side is on the side of the miners most assuredly. There is no class of labor in this country so poorly paid as are the miners of coal and iron ore. They are down at starvation wages all the time. The great companies that own both the mines and the railroads can make coal dear or cheap to the consumer as they please. We had an illustration of that last winter, when the coal companies increased the price of coal to consumers in midwinter nearly 50 cents per ton by simply limiting the output from the mines. In short, they turned labor loose to starve at one end of the line and increased the price of coal to consumers at the other. If labor, however, undertakes to interfere arbitrarily and unjustly with the management of the railroad property, it becomes entirely a different affair. I do not understand that to be the case in the present attitude of the Reading strike.

We have selected the above opinions without regard to politics. We call special attention to the opinions of Representative Brumm, of Pennsylvania, and Senator McPherson, of New Jersey, who are presumed to know better how matters stand than men further away who are more dependent on the misleading dispatches passing over monopoly wires.

The great body of our American congressmen have no opinions on the question at issue, or care nothing about it. Our Kansas senators and representatives, all except Mr. Anderson, are in this deplorable and humiliating condition of ignorance. We give a synopsis of their reported statements as follows:

Senator Ingalls.—I know absolutely nothing about it.

Senator Plumb.—I have nothing to say. I do not consider it in the line of my duties to study the troubles between corporations and their employes.

We beg to suggest right here that in all these and similar troubles, there are three parties in interest: the corporations, the employes, and the public! And the public, with all its business and personal interests and comforts at stake, is, usually, the greatest suffer. If Senator Plumb represents none of these interests, in heaven's name let him resign and give place to some senator who has a juster idea of the "line of his duties!"

Mr. Perkins.—I do not think there was any justification or occasion for the strike.

Mr. Funston.—I have nothing to say about it.

Mr. Morrill.—It is very rarely that the right is entirely on one side, but in this present case I am not prepared to answer the question.

Mr. Ryan.—I am not acquainted with the facts and cannot express an opinion.

Mr. Peters.—I am not sufficiently conversant with the facts to express an opinion.

Mr. Turner.—I have not studied the question.

In short, every senator and representative from Kansas, except the wide-awake and patriotic representative from the Fifth district, was caught and publicly photographed with his finger in his mouth, while the great country they represent and pretend to serve was in urgent need of their attention and services. Hundreds of thousands of the most worthy and the most helpless people were suffering the pangs of cold and hunger; and every northern state, including Kansas, was suffering loss and discomfort for want of their just and usual supply of fuel. Yet none of these men knew or cared anything about it! This is what comes of sending corporation attorneys, bankers, monopolists and speculators to Congress. They have no sympathy with the common people, nor with the legitimate industries of the country. If they are not utterly lost to all sense of shame, their disgraceful nudity of information on a great practical subject thus photographed in the eyes of a disgusted and sorely wronged people, should cause their brazen cheeks to tingle with remorse! Nero could fiddle while Rome burned. Our rich senators and representatives can sleep while millions of our people freeze and starve, under the heels of the coal barons and corporate monopolies that rob and ruin the country at will.

The first practical help comes from the representative of the Fifth Kansas district, in the shape of a resolution of inquiry as to the cause of the continued failure of the Reading railroad to run its trains. Mr. Anderson's resolution was at once accorded a respectful hearing, and every patriot must hope that much good will come of it.

There is said to exist in some of those mining valleys of Pennsylvania more degradation and suffering than were ever seen on the cotton and sugar plantations of the South in the blackest and darkest days of chattel slavery. Let Mr. Anderson's inquiry be permitted, and let it go on with vigor. A flood of light on the subject is what is first wanted. And, as usual, Kansas is to the front! The Fifth district forever ! ! But over the other districts, and over our senators, let us draw the mantle of shameful oblivion !"—*Junction City (Kan.) Tribune, Jan. '88.*

"Since the dawn of history, the great thoroughfares have belonged to the people, have been known as the king's highways or the public highways, and have been open to the free use of all, on payment of a small uniform tax or toll to keep them in repair. But now the most perfect and by far the most important roads known to mankind are owned and managed as private property by a comparatively small number of private citizens. . . . The corporations have become conscious of their strength and have entered upon the work of controlling the states.

Already they have captured several of the oldest and strongest of them; and these discrowned sovereigns (States) now follow in chains the triumphal Chariots of their Conquerers. The modern barons, more powerful than their military prototypes, own our greatest highways and levy tribute at will upon all our vast industries."—*Extract from a speech by James A. Garfield, in 1874.*

"I repeat to-day in substance words uttered seven years ago, that, 'there are in this country four men, who, in the matter of taxation, possess and frequently exercise powers which neither congress nor any state legislature would dare to exert—powers which, if exercised in Great Britain, would shake the throne to the foundation. These men may at any time, and for any reason satisfactory to themselves, by a stroke of the pen, reduce the value of property in the United States by hundreds of millions. They may at their own will and pleasure embarrass business, depress one city or locality and build up another, enrich one individual and ruin his competitors, and when complaint is made coolly reply, "What are you going to do about it?" . . . The channels of commerce being owned and controlled by one man or a few men, what is to restrain corporate power or to fix a limit to its exactions upon the people? What is to hinder these men from depressing or inflating the values of all kinds of property, to suit their caprice or avarice, and thereby gathering into their own coffers the wealth of the nation? Where is the limit to such a power as this? And what

shall be said of the spirit of a free people who will submit without a protest to be thus bound hand and foot!''
—*Senator Windom.*

A very famous writer says: '' To encourage a single bunting factory the very ensign of an American ship has been subjected to a duty of 150 per cent. From keelson to truck, from the wire in her stays to the brass in her taffrail log, everything that goes to the building, the fitting, or the storing of a ship is burdened with heavy taxes. Even should she be repaired abroad she must pay taxes for it on her return home. Thus has protection strangled an industry in which with free trade we might still have led the world. And the injury we have done ourselves has been, in some degree at least, an injury to mankind. Who can doubt that ocean steamers would to day have been swifter and better had American builders been free to compete with English builders?

''Though our navigation laws, which forbid the carrying of a pound of freight or a single passenger from American port to American port on any other than an American-built vessel, obscure the effects of protection in our coasting trade, they are just as truly felt in our ocean trade. The increased cost of building and running vessels has, especially as to steamers, operated to stunt the growth of our coasting trade and to check by higher freights the development of other industries. And how restriction strengthens monopoly is seen in the manner in which the effect of protection upon our coastwise trade has been to make easier the extortions of railway syndicates. For instance, the Pacific Railway pool has for years paid the Pacific Mail Steamship company $85,000 a month to keep up its rates of fare and freight between New York and San Francisco. It would have been impossible for the railway ring thus to prevent competition had the trade between the Atlantic and Pacific been open to foreign vessels."—*Chicago Times, April 21, 1888.*

"The present freight rates on corn were made when corn was selling at 55 cents in Kansas City. Corn is now 15 cents, which leaves a comparative rate of profit four times as large for railroads as for farmers, hence railroads report this the most profitable year in their history, but alas ! for the farmer."—*The Topeka Jeffersonian, January 23d, 1890.*

No Whiskers or No Work.

In compliance with a general order issued by the superintendent of the Philadelphia and Reading Railroad Company, the brakemen and baggage-masters employed on the road will be compelled to report for duty in the future with clean-shaven faces. This order has caused no end of talk among the men, many of whom have beards remarkable for grace and beauty. It is simply a case of whiskers and no work or steady employment and no whiskers.

A number of employes who enjoyed the luxury of a clean shave are now suffering with the grippe. In connection with the order doing away with beards is an order compelling the men to keep their coats closely

buttoned while on duty. This means for the men a
sort of Russian bath between stations,

When the superintendent of the road issued his
sweeping order for the sacrifice of the beards he made
no explanation, but it is generally understood that his
idea is to have all the men employed on the Reading
road look as slick as possible. According to his way
of thinking a man cannot meet these requirements except by having a clean-shaven face.—*New York Herald, 1890.*

"We are asked every few days what in thunder a
trust is. A trust is a regular she-devil, a son-of-a-gun,
a devil-fish. The harder you try to get away the
tighter it fastens on ; it never gets tired, never rests,
never sleeps, has no heart to feel or soul to save ; but is
a stem-winder to do business, and goes through the
farmer's wealth and laborer's pocket quicker than a
dose of salts through a tin horn. The trust staid at
home, shaved notes, bought bonds, run national banks,
and plundered the government while the soldiers were
suppressing the rebellion. The trusts succeed in paying the soldier fifty cents on the dollar, and themselves
from $1.00 to $2.85 in greenbacks for their gold dollar,
which they exchanged for government bonds at par ;
when they had the thing corralled to suit them, they
formed pools and combinations on grain, cattle, beef,
hogs, pork, sugar, flour, coffee, tea, dry goods, groce-
ries, lumber, nails—in fact, anything their fancy might
dictate, and set a price at which the articles should be
sold, and either bought out, run out or crushed out

the smaller dealers; and then the harvest of the trust
came, in the enhanced price for wheat the laborer pur-
chased, and the low price at which the farmer had to
sell, with the lowering of wages, a high protective
tariff for the trusts, and the consumer with a very low
tariff protection or no protection at all—such are
trusts."—*Junction City* (*Kan.*) *Tribune.*

THE HOD-CARRIER'S PRAYER.

Commenting on a lecture by Rev. Dr. Harris before
a well-fed, well-dressed audience in Sidney, N. S. W.,
John Ramsey, writing in the Australian *Standard*
under the nom de plume of "Yasmar," quotes this
passage :

Work on, do the work provided, whether work of
brain or hand, as a God-given task. Work, work,
work ; pray, pray, pray.

To this Mr. Ramsey makes the following sarcastic
reply :

Most excellent advice, and most necessary for the
citizen of Darling Point. His is the work of the brain,
in writing out receipts for the rent of his rows of
houses in the fever plots of the slums, in supervising
the laying out of his grounds by the landscape gar-
dener, and in planning legislative schemes to induce
everybody to be content with his lot. But he is apt
to do these things in a perfunctory way, and needs to
be spurred on to a sense of his duty. And so it is with
the hod-carrier. He is too ready to hang about the
statue, and go to sleep in the park, when he should be

working.   When he knows that he has a delicate wife
at home who is doing her share of work by washing
three days a week, and ironing till midnight, for other
people, in addition to her own house duties, and that
his two little girls are selling matches around the bars
and theatre doors till eleven o'clock every night, and
that his boys are loafing about the wharves all day
picking up bits of coal and chips for the fire, he ought
certainly to engage in some occupation.   Whatever
kind of work it may be, let him remember it is a God
given task.   If he cannot get employment at carrying
bricks and mortar up a forty-foot ladder his pride must
not prevent him from working at some less congenial
task.   Let him go into the country—and he need not
go far, as there is plenty of unused agricultural land
near Sydney—and settle down to a rural life. With his
brawny arms and broad shoulders he could surely raise
enough food to fill the mouths that depend upon him.
But whether he carries bricks or digs potatoes, let him
not neglect to pray.   He may choose the most convenient time for praying, but, as it would probably interfere with the progress of the building, and with the
amount of wages to be received at the end of the week,
to engage in prayer during the day, the most fitting
time would perhaps be before going to bed.   Then,
having given his sick wife the cup of watery gruel
which a poorer neighbor has sent in, and having coaxed
his hungry little children to sleep by the promise of a
big dinner next day, he may proceed to offer up some
such petition as this: "Oh, thou invisible and all
puissant director of the universe, thou beneficent father

of all, as I have been led to believe, permit me, one of thy most insignificant children, to approach thee. I am unworthy to come into thy august presence, and intrude my petty affairs on thy notice seeing that thou art so occupied with the suggestions of the late church congress, the election of a bishop of Sydney, and the reiterated supplications in a popular tune on behalf of the queen of England. I am conscious of the dread consequences which would follow if I presumed so to address an earthly monarch, but though thou art King of kings, I beseech I may be pardoned for approach-ing thee as father.

Thou hast created all things and hast ordained everything to thy pleasure. Thou hast created the great estates of the land syndicate, and the broad park lands of the rich man, which are capable of growing thousands of tons of wheat, and of depasturing tens of thousands of sheep and cattle, and thou has also cre-ated the pangs of hunger which rack my little ones daily ; thou hast ordained the debility and melancholy which heavy toil and want of food have brought to my poor wife, and thou hast created the fortifying beef tea and the blood-giving claret ; thou hast created the typhoid germ, and the hot fever tide which rushes through the veins of my dear little boy, and thou hast also created the drug quinine which sells at one pound an ounce ; thou hast created the costly orchid of the rich man which he has no time to admire, and thou hast also created the geranium in the jam tin on the window sill which cheers my sick loved ones ; thou hast created the kind rich man who builds houses and

gives me the work to do because he is not strong
enough to carry bricks up a ladder, and thou hast created me strong and muscular above all hod-carriers.
Thy ways are inscrutable, but I know thou has or-
dered all things well. It is popularly supposed that
thou hast given man dominion over the field, but I
know this passage is not to be read literally, and refers
to some men only. It is also considered that the
earth is the Lord's, and the fullness thereof, but it is
evident that, for some wise purpose of thine own, thou
hast permitted vast tracts of it to fall into the absolute
possession of a few men, possibly because they are
purer in heart and more humble than I, thy unworthy
creature. Thou being the Great Father of all, these
men are my brethren, but in thine own wise discretion
thou hast deemed it meet that they should retain dominion over my bit of the field, and to that end thou
hast ordained the sacred ordinance of private property
in land. To my blind stubborn intellect it might
seem better that the broad untilled acres of the earth
should produce food for the millions of thy starving
children than be devoted to the deer and the fox and
the racehorse, but I know that all these things shall
be made clear to me in Paradise when I shall be introduced to my brethren, the marquis of Westminster
and Mr. Vanderbilt, and Sir Daniel Cooper, and the
marquis of Argyle, and I, with others like myself,
shall then be able to express our gratitude to them
for the chastening influence they exerted on us on
earth. Therefore I beseech thee that I may always
keep my strength in order to be able to carry bricks,

and that I may never grow old and feeble, as the kind, rich man would then be obliged to carry his own bricks."— *The Standard, November 16, 1889.*

Three Hundred Million Dollars.

———

Curious Calculations Concerning this Enormous Sum of Money.

Philadelphia *Press:* F. H. Swords, a banker of London, sat in the Continental corridor recently reading a newspaper. Suddenly he pointed to a paragraph in the latter and said :

"Listen to this statement: 'The Vanderbilt estate is now calculated to be worth at least $300,000,000.'" Mr. Swords folded his paper, and, leaning back in the chair, continued : "Of course I do not know whether that statement is true ; but I saw it published in the *Standard* several weeks ago.

"The sum seemed so enormous that I spent quite a while in calculating the physical proportions of that number of silver dollars. Here is a little slip in my wallet here that may give you some idea. If Adam, when he first looked around in the Garden of Eden, say 6,000 years ago, had been met by Satan and had been employed by him at a regular salary of $50,000 per annum and his board and clothes ; and if Adam had carefully laid his silver dollars away in barrels each year, and had lived to the present time, he would now have $300,000,000. Again, if a man born in the Christian era, 1890 years ago, had lived and been steadily employed at a salary of $14,000 per month, $443 per day, and his living expenses besides, and had saved every dollar of it, he would not to-day have three hundred millions.

"If it were necessary to transport this number of silver dollars it would require five hundred and thirty-six freight cars each of a capacity of twenty tons. If these cars were put into one train it would be more than four miles long. If it were possible for three hundred million silver dollars to be laid on the ground in a straight line, with edges touching each other the whole distance, the line would reach farther than from London across the Atlantic Ocean and over the North American Continent to San Francisco. A sidewalk of three hundred million silver dollars could be laid six feet wide and more than fifteen miles long. If three hundred million dollars were laid one on top of the other they would make a column 475 miles high. If taken down and arranged in the form of a cube each side of the latter would be thirty-five feet long and wide, and it would weigh more than 10,000 tons. If such a weight were dropped from the roof of the new city hall the concussion would be great enough to destroy that part of the city."—*January 19, 1890.*

"What are you going to do about it?"

"The public be damned!"—*Vanderbilt.*

WHO OWNS AMERICA?

OUR PUBLIC DOMAIN.

A RECORD OF ROBBERY UNPARALLELED IN THE WORLD'S HISTORY.

Even those who have given considerable thought and study to the land qustion and are familiar with the means by which our vast public domain has been frittered away have hardly any adequate conception of the extent to which the people have permitted themselves to be robbed.

All those who are at all interested in this subject should have heard the speech of H Martin Williams, of Missouri, at the Trades Assembly Hall last Saturday night.

The statistics and facts presented by him were a revelation to those who heard him, and he has kindly permitted us to lay them before the readers of *The Jeffersonian.*

They will furnish food for thought and ammunition for those who have the disposition and ability to use them.

LAND GRANTS TO RAILROADS.

From September 20, 1850, to May 4, 1870, one hundred and sixty acts of Congress were passed granting lands to railroads, as follows:

The States in which lands were granted, date of act
of granting same, road to which granted and number
of acres, are:

Illinois, Sept. 20, 1850, Ill. Cent. and Mobile &
    Chicago................................... 2,595,053

Mississippi, Sept. 20, 1850, Mobile & Ohio River.... 1,004,640
Mississippi, Aug. 11, 1856, Vicksburg & Meridian
    Road 404,800
Mississippi, Aug. 11, 1836, Gulf & Ship Island.,.... 652,800

    Total in Mississippi..................... 2,068.240

Alabama, Sept. 50, 1850, Mobile & Ohio River....... 230,400
Alabama · May 17, 1855, Alabama & Florida......... 419,520
Alabama, June 3, 1866, and May 23, 1872, Selma,
    Rome & Dalton............................ 581,920
Alabama, June 3, 1856, Coosa & Tennessee 132,880
Alabama, June 3, 1856, Mobile & Girard........... 840,880
Alabama, June 3, 1856, and April 18, 1689, Alabama
    & Chattanooga............................ 879,920
Alabama, June 3, 1855, and March 3, 1871, South &
    North Alabama........................... 576.100

    Total in Alabama......................... 3,579,00

Florida, May 17, 1856 Florida Railroad............. 442.542
Florida, May 17, 1856. Florida & Alabama......... 165.688
Florida, May 17, 1856, Pensacola & Georgia........ 1,568,729
Florida, May 17, 1856, Florida, Atlantic & Gulf...... 183.153

    Total in Florida......................... 2,360,112

Louisiana, June 3, 1856, Vicksburg & Shreveport.... 610,880
Louisiana, June 3, 1856, and July 14, 1870, N. O., Op-
    elousas & Gt. West...................... 967,840

    Total in Louisiana....................... 1,578,720

Arkansas, Feb, 9, 1853, July 28, 1866, May 6, 1870,
   Cairo & Fulton.... ....   1,160.667
Arkansas, Feb. 9, 1855, July 28, 1866, April 10. 1869,
   March 8, 1870, Little Rock & Fort Smith......   1009,290
Arkansas, July 4, 1866, Iron Mountain............   864,000
                                                   ──────────
      Total in Arkansas........................   4,878,148

Missouri, June 10, 1852, Hannibal and St. Jo........   781,944
Missouri, June 10, 1852, Pacific & West Branch.....   1,161,235
Missouri, Feb. 9, 1853, Cairo & Fulton............   219,262
Missouri, July 28, 1856, Cairo & Fulton...........   182,718
Missouri, July 29, 1866, St. Louis & Iron Mountain.   640,000
                                                     ──────────
      Total in Missouri.........................   2,985,159

Iowa, May 5, 1856, June 2, 1864, Feb. 10, 1866, Bur-
   lington & Missouri River....................   948,643
Iowa, May 15, 1856, June 2, 1864, Jan. 31, 1873, Chi-
   cago, Rock Island & Pacific..................   1,261,181
Iowa, May 15, 1856, June 2, 1864, Cedar Rapds & Mis-
   souri River.................................   1,298,739
Iowa, May 15, 1856, Iowa Falls & Sioux City.......   1,226,163
Iowa, June 2, 1864, March 2, 1868, May 12, 1864, Du-
   buque and Sioux City and McGregor & Missouri
   River   1,536,000
Iowa, May 12, 1864, Sioux City & St. Paul...... ...   524,800
                                                    ──────────
      Total in Iowa   6,987,526

Michigan, June 3, 1856, Detroit & Milwaukee.......   355,430
Michigan, June 3, 1856, Pt. Huron & Milwaukee...   312,384
Michigan, June 3, 1867, March 2, 1867, March 3, 1871,
   Jackson, Lansing & Saginaw.................   1,052,469
Michigan, June 3, 1856, Feb. 17, 1866, July 3, 1866,
   March 3, 1871, Flint & Pere Marquette........   586,828

Michigan, July 3, 1856, June 7, 1864, March 3, 1866, May 20, 1868, April 20, 1871, Marquette, Houghton & Ontonagon	552,515
July 3, 1856, June 7, 1864, March 3, 1871, Grand Rapids & Indiana	1,160,392
Michigan, March 3, 1865, Bay de Noquet, Marquette & St. Ste. Maria	128,000
Total in Michigan	4,712,478
Wisconsin, June 3, 1856, May 5, 1864, March 3, 1873, West Wisconsin	999,984
Wisconsin, June 3, 1856, May 5, 1864, St. Croix and Lake Superior and Branch to Bayfield	1,408,441
Wisconsin, June 3, 1856, April 25, 1862, May 3, 1855, March 3, 1869, Chicago & Northwestern	600,000
Wisconsin, May 5, 1864, June 21, 1866, Wisconsin Central	750,000
Total in Wisconsin	3,758,434
Minnesota, March 3, 1857, March 3, 1873, St. Paul & Pacific	1,248,638
Minnesota, March 3, 1857, March 3, 1866, July 12, 1862, Branch St. Paul & Pacific	1,475,000
Minnesota, March 3, 1871, March 3, 1873, St. Vincent Branch	643,403
Minnesota, March 13, 1857, July 13, 1866, Jan. 13, 1873, Winona & St. Peters	1,410,000
Minnesota, March 3, 1857, May 12, 1864, St. Paul & Sioux City	1,010,000
Minnesota, May 5, 1864, July 13, 1866, Lake Superior & Mississippi	920,000
Minnesota, July 4, 1866, Southern Minnesota	735,000
Minnesota, July 4, 1865, Hastings & Dakota	550,000
Total in Minnesota	9,892,041

Kansas, March 3, 1863, July 1, 1864, April 19, 1871,
  Leavenworth, Lawrence & Galveston....   800,000
Kansas, March 3, 1863, July 1, 1864, April 19, 1871,
  Missouri, Kansas & Texas....................   1,520,000
Kansas, March 3, 1863, Atchison, Topeka & S. F.....   3,000,000
Kansas, July 23, 1866, St. Jo. & Denver............   1,700,000
Kansas, July 25, 1866, Missouri River, Fort Scott &
  Gulf.. ..   2,350,000
Kansas, July 1, 1862, July 2, 1864, July 3, 1866, May 7,
  1866, March 3, 1869, Kansas Pacific............   6,000,000
          of which 4,000,000 was in Kansas.
Kansas, July 1, 1862, July 20, 1864, Central Branch
  Union Pacific.................................   245,166
                                                   ──────────
      Total in Kansas............................. 20,815,000

To corporations, July 1, 1862, July 2, 1864, July 3,
  1866, July 26, 1866, April 10, 1869, May 6, 1870,
  Union Pacific................................. 12,000,000
To corporations, March 3, 1869, Denver Pacific.....   1,000,000
To corporations, July 1, 1862, July 2, 1864, Central
  Pacific.....................   8,000,000
To corporations, by same acts to Central Pacific, suc-
  cessors by consolidation with Western Pacific....   1,100,000
To corporations, July 2, 1864, Sioux City Pacific....   60,000
To corporations, July 2, 1864, May 7, 1868, July 1,
  1868, March 1, 1869, April 10, 1869, May 31,1870,
  Northern Pacific............................. 47,000,000
To corporations, July 3, 1866, Placerville & Sacra-
  mento.................................. ....   200.000
To corporations, July 26, 1866, June 25, 1868, April
  10, 1869, Oregon Branch of Central Pacific......   3,000,000
To corporations, July 25, 1866, June 25, 1868, April 10,
  1869, Oregon & California....................   3,500,000
To corporations, July 27, 1866, April 20, 1871, Atlan-
  tic & Pacific............................. 42,000,000

To corporations, July 27, 1866, March 3, 1871, Southern Pacific.................................... 9,520,000
To corporations, March 2, 1867, Stockton & Copper-
opolis ... . ' 320,000
To corporations, May 4, 1870, Oregon Central....... 1,200,000

Total acres land granted to railroads.....,....191,903,957
Or enough to make 1,199,400 farms of 160 acres each.

TOTAL LAND GRANTS.

	Acres.
For canals, from 1827 to 1866....................	4,405,968
For educational purposes.........................	77,493,162
To railroad corporations........	191,903,957

Total amount given away................... 273,803,105

The amount of land is greater by 17,000 square
miles than the combined area of the six New England
States and New York, New Jersey, Delaware, Mary-
land, Pennsylvania, Ohio, Indiana, Illinois, Michigan,
Wisconsin, Iowa and Missouri, or all the States east of
the Mississippi and north of the Ohio Rivers, including all the populous and wealthy states, now contain-
ing forty millions of people, and not yet half settled.

In addition to this, 12,963,593 acres of public lands
have been illegally enclosed by cattle and other syndicates, largely composed of foreign nobles.

ALIEN LAND-OWNERS.

The following foreign individuals and syndicates
own the amount of land set opposite their names :

	Acres.
An English syndicate in Texas....................	3,000,000
Holland Land Company, New Mexico..............	4,500,000

Sir E. Reed, syndicate in Florida.................. 2,000,000
English syndicate in Mississippi....... 1,800,000
Baron Tweedale.. 1,750,000
Phillips, Marshall & Co., London.................. 1,300,000
German syndicate. 1,100,000
Anglo-American syndicate, London................ 750,000
Byron H. Evans, London.......................... 700,000
Duke of Sutherland................................ 422,000
British Land Company in Kansas... 320,000
W. Wharley, M. P., Peterboro.... 310,000
Missouri Land Company, Scotland.............. 300,000
Robert Tenant, of London........................ 530,000
Dundee Land Co., Scotland 247,000
Lord Dunmore........................·.............. 120,000
Bengame Neugas, Liverpool....................... 100,000
Lord Houghton, in Florida 60,000
Lord Dunraven, in Colorado...................... 60,000
English Land Co., Florida......................... 50,000
English Land Co., Arkansas....... ...., 50,000
A. Peel, M. P., Leicestershire, E.................. 10,000
Sir J. L. Kay, Yorkshire, E...................... 5,000
Alexander Grant, London, Kan................... 35,000
English Syndicate, Wisconsin.................. 110,000
M. Ellerhausea, West Virginia.................. 600,000
A Scotch Syndicate in Florida.................... 500,000
A. Boysen, Danish Consul, Mil.................. 50,000
Missouri Land Co., Edinburg.................... 165,000
H. Disston in Florida............................. 2,000,000
Baron Wm. Scully, in Ill. and Kas............... 200,000
Richard Sykes and Mr. Hughes, of England, in Da-
    kota.................................... 85,000
C. M. Beach, of London, in Dakota.............. 10,000
Finlay Dun & Co., in Dakota.................... 25,000
Marquis Demores, in Dakota and Montana.,........ 15,000
Close Brothers.................................... 270,000
Marquis of Aylesbury.. 55,051
Duke of Beaufort.. 51,085

Duke of Bedford........	87,507
Earl of Brownlow.....................	57,799
Earl of Carlisle	70,540
Earl of Cawdor.............................	51,538
Duke of Cleveland.........................	106,650
Earl of Derby...............................	56,598
Maxwell Land Co............................	1,714,964
Duke of Devonshire..................	148,629
Lord Beconsfield............................	66,101
Lord Londesborough........................	52,655
Earl of Lonsdale............................	67,950
Duke of Northumberland.....	191.480
Duke of Portland,...........................	55,259
Earl of Powis...............................	46,095
Duke of Rutland............................	70,039
Lady Willoughby............................	59,912
Sir W. W. Wynn............................	91,032
Earl of Sarborough........	55,370

26,213,354

Here are fifty-six foreign corporations and individuals who own more land than there is in the state of Indiana, by 860,630 acres, or enough to give 140,615 American citizens each a farm of 160 acres.

This list is incomplete, comprising only fifty-six corporations and individuals owning an aggregate of 26,-213,354 acres. A full list of the foreigners who have acquired land in the country, would show an aggregate holding of not less than 40,000,000 acres.

This does not include farms taken by foreign loan companies on foreclosure in the United States courts, which aggregate more acres than all the above large holdings. It was stated in a reliable republican paper about a year ago that over 2,700 farms in northern

Kansas had passed to foreign loan companies by foreclosure in eighteen months.   Neither does this list include the enormous land values in mines and mining
stocks,   rights of way of railroads, etc., owned by
foreigners.

AMERICAN LAND OWNERS.

In presenting the following list of thirty American
corporations and persons owning large bodies of land,
aggregating 14,036,000 acres, Mr. Williams stated
that it constituted but a fraction of the American land
grabbers, and that the. list might be extended indefi-
nitely.

It is generally thought of the American landlord
that he is a very harmless, inoffensive sort of an individual, when, in truth, he is just as bad ; just as greedy;
just as mean and just as dangerous as his twin brother
across the water.   He is simply a separate link of the
same sausage made out of the same dog.

American land lords hold more land in the United
States for speculative purposes and to grow rich from
rent, than is held by foreign land owners in this
country. Here is a partial list, with the amount owned
by each :

	Acres.
Ex-Senator Dorsey, in N. M................	500,000
Col. D. C. Murphy.................................	4,068,000
Col. Church of New York, 180 farms of from 200 to	
500 acres each, in all about....................	60,000
Mr. Clark, of New York.........................	30,000
Standard Oil Co., in several states.................	1,000,000
Dr. Glenn, of California.........................	90,000
E. Mariner, of Milwaukee, Wis.....................	70,000

George Hanley, in Wisconsin	32,000
David Selsor, in Ohio	25.000
Maurice Raleigh, in New Jersey	30,000
E. C. Sprague, in several states	500,000
Virginia Coal & Iron Co.	100,000
Col. Myer, in Wisconsin	35,000
Texas Land & Cattle Co.	240,000
Texas State Fund (owned by four men)	3,000,000
A New York Syndicate, in Texas	300,000
McLaughlin, of California	400,000
Wm. S. Chapman, in California	350,000
Ex-State Surveyor Gen Houghton, of California	35,000
Ex-State Surveyor Gen. Beals	300,000
Miller & Lux, of San Francisco	450,000
John W. Dwight, of Pennsylvania, owns in North Dakota a farm nearly as large as the state of Rhode Island........1100 sq. miles	704,000
Bixby, Flint & Co., of San Francisco	200,000
G. W. Roberts, of San Francisco	140,000
Isaac Freidlander, of California	100,000
Throckmorton, of California	146,000
Murphy family, of Santa Clara	156,000
Thos. Fowler, in California	200,000
Abel Stearns, of Los Angeles	200,000
A Philadelphia firm, in California	200,000
Total	14,036,000

Here we have 29 American corporations and individuals who own 14,036,000 acres, or a good deal more than half as much land as there is within the boundaries of the state of Indiana! And this is only a very small part of the number of American land owners, who hold from 5,000 to 4,000,000 acres each.

WHAT IT MEANS.

Nearly all the great fortunes of America have been derived from these unjust and illegal land grants, and from the increase of land values in cities, towns, villages, mines, forests, and railway and street-car rights of way and other franchises—all of which were the property and inheritance of the whole people until stolen through bribery and corruption of false and traitorous politicians. The United States Senate is principally composed of the beneficiaries of these land grants and their paid satraps and attorneys and the United States House of Representatives is dominated by the same interests and influences. The State officers and legislators of the Western States and territories are the creatures and servants of the men and corporations grown rich and arrogant through land grants and railway franchises, both of which are the birthright and part of the sovereignty of the people and should have been held for the common good of all.

To abolish all other direct or indirect taxes, except possibly that necessary for police control of nuisances, as on whisky, dogs, etc., and to raise all public revenues by a single tax on the rental value of real estate alone, exclusive of improvements, will reclaim to the people their lost inheritance and restore their birthright in the bounties of nature.

Otherwise, we become like Ireland—a nation of proud and haughty landlords and servile and helpless tenants. No palliative nor half-way measures will right the wrong. The axe must be laid to the root of the deadly Upas tree. The poison, miasmatic stream of privilege must be dried up—not turned into a new channel. Are *you* helping or hindering the work of redeeming man from thralldom?"—*The (Topeka, Kan.) Jeffersonian, January 30th, 1890.*

PARNELL'S TRIUMPH.

The friends of Mr. Parnell and all men who love justice and fair play, will rejoice with him in his final triumph over the London *Times*. It has persecuted and vilified him for years, but the persecutions are at an end. The original trial broke down after the suicide of the forger Pigott, and when he turned upon his enemy and sued for libel, warned by past experience, it acknowledged the injustice it had done him and the baseless character of its assaults, as well as its own craven fear, by compromising with him and paying him heavy damages to withdraw the suit. It was a clear case of political persecution and an attempt to drive him from the policy he has pursued so long and so manfully, and it had all the forces of the Tory party at its back helping to break him down, to smash the Home Rule party, and to deal Mr. Gladstone a mortal blow at the same time. The miserable conspiracy has failed, however. Mr. Parnell is vindicated and the Thunderer will have to try some other tactics. It is safe to assume that it will not asperse the great Irish leader again. One of the reasons which inspired the settlement with Mr. Parnell was undoubtedly the *Times'* determination to avoid disclosing under oath its circulation, which has decreased at a rapid rate in recent years."—*Chicago Tribune, Feb. 4th, 1890.*

This is a pure case of pot calling the kettle black, and right here I want to draw an analogy between the attacks upon Mr. Parnell by the London *Times*, in which he was vilified as a conspirator lending counsel to murder even, and the attacks upon the so-called anarchists by the " press " of this country before during and since that travestie upon law which condemned to death four innocent men, for opinion's sake, and three more to a life sentence in Joliet Prison for having uttered truth upon the streets of Chicago.

See pages, 65, 84, 135, 140, and 142.—*G. P. M.*

CLASSICAL OPINIONS

BOTH ANCIENT AND MODERN.

Our laws are very flexible. . . . The laws of the State of Illinois are peculiarly flexible and accommodating."—*Chicago Tribune.*

?   ?   ?   ?   ?

" The populace condemn what they do not understand."—*Cicero.*

"The ultimate tendency of civilization is towards barbarism.."—*Hare.*

"Revolutions are terrible affairs, but they are as necessary as amputation when mortification sets in."
—*Henrich Heine.*

Are not the millionaires rolling and rotting in limberger luxury, indolence and viciousness?—*G. P. M.*

"It is only by making the ruling few uneasy that the oppressed many can obtain a particle of relief."—*Jeremy Bentham.*

"For it so happens that the ease, the luxury, and the abundance of the highest state of civilization are as productive of selfishness as the difficulties, the privations and the sterilties of the lowest."—*Colton.*

"With some the word liberty may mean for each man to do as he pleases with himself and the product of his labor, while with others the same word may mean for some men to do as they please with other men and the product of other men's labor."—*Abraham Lincoln.*

"If we expect the virtues of manhood we must secure the conditions of manhood.—*Heber Newton.*

"Whatever the apparent cause of any riots may be, the real one is always want of happiness. . . . A great part of that order which reigns among mankind is not the effect of government. It had its origin in the principles of society, and the natural constitution of man. It existed prior to government and would exist if the formality of government was abolished. . . . In fine. society performs of itself almost everything which is ascribed to government. . . . . The more perfect civilization is, the less occasion has it for government, because the more does it regulate its own affairs, and govern itself ; but so contrary is the practice of all governments to the reason of the case, that the expenses ef them increase in the proportion they ought to diminish.   It is but few general laws that civilized life requires, and those of such common usefullness, that whether they are enforced by the forms of government or not, the effect will be nearly the same."— *Tom Paine.*

" I pity, execrate and hate the man who has only to brag that he is white. . . . Liberty, Fraternity, Equality—these three grandest words in all the languages of men.   Liberty :   Give to every man the fruit of his own labor.   Fraternity : Every man in the right is my brother.   Equality : The rights of all men are equal. . . .   When you stop free speech, when you say that a thought shall die in the womb of the brain, it would have the same effect upon the intellectual world that to stop springs at their sources would have upon the physical world.   I have always said that the more liberty there is given away, the more liberty you have.—*Robert Ingersoll.*

The landlords of England have ruled it six hundred years, the corporations of America mean to rule it in the same way, and unless some power more radical than that of ordinary politics is found, will rule it inevitably. . . . .   No civil society, no government can exist except on the basis of the willing submission of all its citizens, and by the performance of the duty of rendering equal justice between man and man. Whatever calls itself a government, and refuses that duty, or has not that assent, is no government. It is only a pirate ship. . . . . This is historically true—that no reform, moral or intellectual, ever came down from the upper classes of society. Each and all come up from the protest of martyr and victim. In other words, as Byron expressed it : " Who would be free themselves must strike the blow."—*Wendell Phillips.*

"The destitute laborer might better be a slave than free, for the slave must be supported by his master, while the free laborer is left to starve."—*Judge T. M. Cooley.*

"A nation is to seek the greatest good of all, not of the greatest number ; not to sacrifice the minority to the majority, nor one single man to the whole."— *Theodore Parker.*

"Everything in the universe is bought and sold, and why not wind? . . . . The earth is rented from its surface down to its central mines. . . . . The fire and the means of feeding it are currently bought and sold. . . . The wretches that sweep the boisterous ocean with their nets pay ransom for the privilege of being drowned in it. . . . What title has the air to be exempted from the universal curse of traffic? . . . . In many countries the priests will sell you a portion of heaven. . . . ,

In all countries men are willing to buy in exchange
for health, wealth and peace of conscience, a full allowance of hell."—*Sir Walter Scott.*

"Every actual state is corrupt. . . . . Every
child that is born must have a just chance for its bread.
. . . . We live in a very low state of the world,
and pay willing tribute to a government founded on
force. . . . . The less government the better—
the fewer laws the less confided power. . . . .
People do not seem to think that society can be maintained without artificial restraints, or that the private
citizen might be reasonable and a good neighbor, without the hint of a jail or confiscation. . . . . A
man who cannot be acquainted with me ; looking from
afar, ordains that a part of my labor shall go to the
government, that whimsical end, not as I, but as he
happens to fancy. Behold the consequences. Of all
debts, men are the less willing to pay taxes. What a
satire is this upon government ! everywhere they seem
to think they get their money's worth except for
these. . .   I own I have little esteem for governments. . . . . Of course the timid and base
persons, all who are conscious of no worth in themselves, and who owe all their place to the opportunities under the old order of things which allows them
to deceive and defraud men, shudder at a change, and
would silence every honest voice, and lock up every
house where liberty and innovation can be pleaded
for. They would raise mobs, for fear is very cruel. .
. . . If we look wider, things are all alike; laws

and letters and creeds and modes of living seem a travestie of truth.

Our society is encumbered by ponderous machinery,
which resembles the endless acqueducts which the
Romans built over hill and dale, and which are su-
perceded by the discovery of the law that water rises
to the level of its source. It is a Chinese wall that
any nimble Tartar can leap over. It is a standing
army, not so good as a peace. It is a graduated,
titled, richly appointed Empire quite superfluous when
Town-meetings are found to answer just as well."—
Ralph Waldo Emerson.

" A man with $1,000,000 a year eats the whole fruit
of 5,656 men's labor through a year, for you can get a
stout spadesman to work and maintain himself for the
sum of $150.   Thus we have private individuals whose
wages are equal to the wages of 7,000 or 8,000 individuals.   What do those highly benefited individuals
do to society for their wages? Kill partridges ! Can
this last ? No ; by the soul that is in man, it cannot
and shall not. . . . . A man willing to work
and unable to find work is perhaps the saddest sight
that fortune's inequality exhibits under the sun. . .
. . That he might be put on a level with the four-
footed workers on the planet which is his ! There is
not a horse willing to work but can get his food and
shelter in requital ; a thing this two-footed worker has
to seek for, to solicit for occasionally in vain. And
yet it is currently reported that the two-footed worker
has an immortal soul within him."—*Thomas Carlyle.*

"The root of socialism in its malignant (?) form is the idea that the vast mass of men have the same rights as those at the top. They have not! They have the right to live, the primary conditions of life are universal ; but the right to all the things belonging to civilization depends upon what a man is. The man who is merely bone and muscle has no right to that kind ; he has a right to fodder, certainly."— *Henry Ward Beecher.*

Was blasphemy ever more fiendish? Was a heart ever much blacker, ever filled with more putrid corruption? This wrecker—this wicked scandal maker, this so-called preacher at a salary of $40,oco. Where is he now? Is not the bone and muscle of one man as dear to himself and to the nation as is the so-called brains of some others ? If not then there is no virtue in the teaching of Jesus Christ, nor in society, nor in governments ; and wherein we expect little virtue in governments, we do expect it of individuals, especially of those who are "on top." But how came these individuals "on top" and how did they get there, honestly? I doubt it, and being there, what virtue did they ever hand down to "the vast mass of men" who earned the bread they consumed to feed and cram the brains with vicious vituperations, to find utterance years after to the applause of our so-called Society ?— *Geo. P. McIntyre.*

"The good are better made by ill ;
As odors crushed are sweeter still."
—*Samuel Rogers.*

" Men are starving to death under our civilization of to-day, and it is only in civilized society that men starve to death."—*John G. Huhn.*

Now it is important to enquire whether it is not in the nature of uncontrolled power always to abuse itself. For my part I have no doubt of it, and should as soon see the power that could arrest a stone in falling, proceed from the stone itself as to trust force within any defined limits. I should like to be shown a country where slavery has been abolished by voluntary action of the masters."—*Bastiat.*

" Congress shall make no law abridging the freedom of speech or of press. It is neither more or less . . . . than that every man shall be at liberty to publish what is true, with good motives and for justifiable ends. And. . . . it is not only right in itself, but it is an inestimable privilege in a free government. . . . . No one can doubt the importance in a free government of a right to canvass the acts of public men, and the tendency of public measures, to censure boldly the conduct of rulers, and scrutinize closely the policy and plans of the government. If we would preserve it, public opinion must be enlightened ; political vigilance must be inculcated ; free, but not licentious discussion, must be encouraged."—*Story, on Constitution, Vol. 2, page 667, Section 1880.*

" Upon a large survey of the whole subject, he has not scrupled to declare that :   " It has become a constitutional principle in this country, that every citizen may freely speak, write and publish his sentiments, *being responsible for the abuse of that right ;* and that no law can rightfully be passed to restrain or abridge the freedom of the press."—*Mr. Chancellor Kent.*

VICTOR HUGO.

His Remarkable Address to the Rich and Poor.

His Most Precious Legacy to Humanity.

One Message to the Rich, the Other to the Poor.

The *Sum of Human Wisdom..*

"I am asked what has been the lesson of my life, which I have learned in my years of living to bequeath as my most precious legacy to humanity. I reply that my soul has two messages of counsel, of promise and of threat, to deliver. One to the rich, the other to the poor. The two contain the sum of human wisdom.

To The Rich :

The poor cry out to the wealthy. The slaves implore their rulers. And as much now as in the days of Spartan Helots. I am one of them and I add my

voice to that of the multitude that it may reach the
ears of the rich. Who am I? One of the people.
From whence come I? From the bottomless pit. How
am I named? I am Wretchedness. My lords, I have
something to say to you. My lords, you are placed
high. You have power, opulence, pleasure, the sun
immovable at your zenith, unlimited authority, enjoy-
ment undivided, a total forgetfulness of others. So
be it. But there is something below you. Above you,
perhaps. My lords, I impart to you a novelty. The
human race exists. I am he who comes from the depths.
My lords, you are the great and the rich. That is
perilous. You take advantage of the night. But
have a care; there is a greater power, the morning.
The dawn cannot be vanquished. It will come. It
comes. It has within it the outbreak of irresistible
day. You, you are the dark clouds of privilege. Be
afraid. The true master is about to knock at the door.
What is the father of privilege? Chance. What is
his son? Abuse. Neither chance nor abuse is enduring.
They have, both of them, an evil to-morrow. I come
to warn you. I come to denounce you your own bliss.
It is made out of the ills of others. Your paradise
is made out of the hell of the poor. I come to open
before you, the wealthy, the grand assizes of the poor
—that sovereign who is the slave, that convict who is
the judge. I am bowed down under what I have to
say. Where to begin? I know not. I have picked
up in the cruel experience of suffering, my vast though
struggling pleas. Now what shall I do with them?

They overwhelm me and I throw them forth, pell-
mell before me.

I am a diver, and I bring up from the depths a pearl,
the Truth.   I speak because I know, I have experienced.   I have seen.   Suffering?   No, the word is
weak, O masters in bliss !   Poverty—I have grown up
in it ; winter—I have shivered in it ; famine—I have
tasted it ; scorn—I have undergone it ; the plague—I
have had it; shame—I have drunk of it.   I felt it
requisite that I should come among you.   Why?
because of my yesterday's rags.   It was in order that
my voice might be raised among the satiated, that God
coming—led me with the hungered.   Oh ! you know
not this fatal world, whereto you believe that you belong.   So high, you are outside of it.   I will tell you
what it is.   Abandoned, an orphan, alone in boundless creation, I made my entry into this gloom that
you call society.   The first thing I saw was law, under the form of a gibbet ; the second was wealth—it is
your wealth under the form of a woman dead of cold
and hunger ; the third was luxury under the shape of
a hunted man chained to prison walls; the fourth was
your palaces beneath the shadow of which cowered
the tramp.   The human race has been made by you
slaves and convicts.   You have made of this earth a
dungeon.   Light is wanting, air is wanting, virtue is
wanting.   The workers of this world whose fruits you
enjoy, live in death.   There are little girls who begin
at eight by prostitution, and who end at twenty by
old age.

Who of you have been to Newcastle-on-Tyne? There are men in the mines who chew coal, to fill the stomach and cheat hunger. Look you to Lancashire. Misery everywhere. Are you aware that the Harlech fisshermen eat grass when the fishery fails? Are you aware that at Burton Lazers there are still certain lepers driven into the woods who are fired at if they come out of their dens? In Peckridge there are no beds in the hovels, and holes are dug in the ground for little children to sleep in ; so that in place of beginning with the cradle they begin with the tomb. Mercy, have mercy for the poor? Oh ! I conjure you, have pity ! But no, you will not. I KNOW YE ALL ; DEVILS BRED IN HELL AND DOGS WITH HEARTS OF STONE. Upward to your golden thrones FOR AGES HAS GONE THE CRY OF MISERY, the groan of hunger and the sob of despair, AND YE HEARD IT NOT. What mercy thou hast given shall be meted out to you in turn. Bear in mind that the series of Kings armed with the sword was interrupted by Cromwell with an ax. Tremble ! The incorruptible dissolutions draw near ; the clipped talons push out again ; the torn out tongues take to flight, become tongues of flame scattered to the wings of darkness, and they howl in the Infinite. They who are hungry show their idle teeth. Paradises built over hells, totter. There is suffering, there is suffering, and that which is above leans over, and that which is below gaps open. The shadow asks to become light. The damned discuss the elect. It is the people who are on-coming. I tell you it is MAN who ascends,

It is the end that is beginning.   It is the red dawn-
ing of Catastrophe.   Ah ! this society is false.   One
day, and soon, the true society will come.   Then there
will be no more lords ; there will be free, living men.
There will be no more wealth, there will be abundance
for the poor.   There will be no more masters, but
there will be brothers.   They that toil shall have.
This is the future.   No more prostration, no more
abasement, no more ignorance, no more wealth, no
more beasts of burden, no more courtiers, no more
kings—but LIGHT.

To The Poor.

Shall I now speak to the poor after having in vain
implored the rich ?   Yes, it is fitting.   This, then, have
I to say to the disinherited :   Keep a watch on your
abominable jaw.

There is one rule for the rich—to do nothing, and
one for the poor—to say nothing.   The poor have but
one friend, silence.   They should use but one mono-
syllable :   Yes.   To confess and to concede—this is all
the "rights" they have.   "Yes," to the judge.
"Yes," to the king.   The great, if it so please them
give us blows with a stick ; I have had them ; it is
their prerogative, and they lose nothing of their greatness in cracking our bones.   Let us worship the scepter which is the first among sticks.   If a poor man is
happy he is the pick-pocket of happiness.   Only the
rich and noble are happy by right.   The rich man is
he who being young, has the rights of old age ; being
old, the lucky chances of youth ; vicious, the respect

of good people; a coward, the command of the stout-hearted; doing nothing, the fruits of labor. Carriages, poor slave, exist. The Lord is inside ; the people are under the wheel ; the wise man makes room. The people fight. Whose is the glory? The kings. They pay. Whose is the magnificence? The kings. And the people like to be rich in this fashion. Our ruler, King or Crossus, receive from the poor a crown piece, and renders back to the poor a farthing. How generous he is! The collossal pedestal looks up to the pigmy superstructure. How tall the mankin is! He is on my back. A dwarf has an excellent method of being higher than a giant, it is to perch himself upon the other's shoulders. But that the giant should let him do it, there's the odd part of it; and that he should admire the baseness of the dwarf, there's the stupidity. Human ingenuousness!

The equestrian statue, reserved for Kings alone is an excellent type of royalty. Let us be frank with words. The Capitalists who steals the reward of labor is a king as well as the man of blood. The king mounts himself on the horse. The horse is the people. Sometimes this horse transfigures himself by degrees. At the beginning he is an ass; at the end he is a lion. Then he throws his rider to the ground and we have 1643 in England and 1789 in France; and sometimes he devours him, in which case we have in England 1649 and in France 1793. That the lion can again become a jackass, this is surprising but a fact. What happiness to be again ridden and beaten and starved. What happiness to work for ever for bread and water!

" What happiness to be free from the delusions that cake is good, and life other than misery ! Was there anything more crazy than those ideas? Where should we be if every vagabond had his rights? Imagine everybody governing ! Can you fancy a city directed by the men who built it? They are the team not the coachman. What a God-send is a rich man who takes charge of everything: Surely he is generous to take this trouble for us ! And then he was brought up to it ; he knows what it is ; it is his business. A guide is necessary for us. Being poor we are ignorant ; being ignorant we are blind ; we need a guide. But why are we ignorant? Because it must be so. Ignorance is the guardian of VIRTUE ! He who is ignorant is innocent ! It is not our duty to think, complain or reason. These truths are uncontestable. SO- CIETY reposes on them. What is "society?" Misery for you if you support it. Death if you dare touch it. Be reasonable, poor man, you were made to be a slave. *Not to be a slave is to* dare *and* do."— *Victor Hugo.*

BEFORE THE WAR,

AS WAS

Wm. Lloyd Garrison,
Wendell Phillips,
Martyrs Lovejoy and Brown,
Harriet Beecher Stowe,
Abraham Lincoln,
And many others in conviction,
So am I.

DURING THE WAR IN WAYS AND MEANS
AND SINCE THEN, AS WAS

Peter Cooper,
Wendell Phillips,
Thad. Stevens,
Judge William Kelley,
Henry Wilson,
Salmon P. Chase,
D. P. Mitchell,
W. H. T. Wakefield,
John Davis,
And tens of thousands other illustrious men,
So was and am I.

IN GOVERNMENTS,

AS WAS, AND ARE.

Socrates,
Plato,
Archimedes,
Mazzini,
Voltaire,
Oliver Cromwell,
"Junius,"
Tom Paine,
Walter Scott,
Patrick Henry,
Henrich Heine,
Thomas Carlyle,
Victor Hugo,
Herbert Spencer,
J. S. Mill,
Thomas Jefferson,
Ralph Waldo Emerson,
Wendell Phillips,
Robert Ingersoll,
W. H. T. Wakefield,
Hugh O. Pentecost,
David Overmyer,
George C. Clemens,
Samuel Gompers,
P. G. McGuyre,
John Most,
Burnette G. Haskell,
Frank Q. Stewart,

Benj. R. Tucker,
W. C. Owens,
George A. Schilling,
Lawrence Gronlund,
Dyer D. Lum,
William Holmes,
Albert R. Parson,
August Spies,
Louis Lingg,
Oscar W. Neebe,
Adolph Fischer,
Michael Schawb,
George Engel,
Samuel Fielden,

And thousands upon tens of thousands others " salt of the earth," these would I emulate, for as these were and are so am I.

" God moves not otherwise.   There is no new birth,
But has its corresponding throes of agony ;
The labor pains of all the teeming earth
But shape the course of Destiny !"—*Anonymous.*

THE END.

SLAVERY.

While I now this "proof" am reading,
   Softly through the open door,
Comes a melody revealing,
   The confessions of the poor—
And the words so fraught with meaning,
   Stir my manhood till it whirls
Into maddened frenzy, streaming
   From my eyes, for these poor girls;
Who are singing, sighing, singing
   Mournfully with rhythmic stress,
Keeping time to the clatter and the rattle of the press,
   And those mournful words are ringing,
   Whilst the great machinery whirls—
*Ah, "there's nothing *left* but slavery for poor *honest*
   working girls.

---

* Words italicised are the author's.—February 4th, 1890.

MRS. GEO. P. McINTYRE, PUBLIC READER,
CHICAGO, ILL.

———

THE ANNOUNCEMENT.

FIRST VOICE.

Through my wife will I speak to the people
  Of the wrongs which burthen the poor ;
Until few are the homes where laughter may come.
  Because of "The wolf at the door."

SECOND VOICE.

For the goodness of Truth will I utter
  The burthens which fetter the poor ;
In the Hope that all greed from the earth may recede,
  And with it "The WOLF FROM the door !"

BOTH VOICES.

As helpmeets together we labor,
  In behalf of the sorrowing poor ;
In the Faith that the day is not far away,
  When the "Wolf" will be THRUST from each door.

ACKNOWLEDGEMENTS.

I take pleasure in acknowledging the obligations I am under to Mr. Edgar S. Werner, 48 University Place, N. Y., Publisher of that most worthy compilation, "Elocutionary Studies and New Recitations," (By Mrs. Anna Randall Deihl), from which was taken "The Voice of the People," the author of which mention is made under the heading 'Dedicatory.' And, also to my friend, Wm. Holmes, whose Scrap-book I found invaluable in this compilation. And to my wife, ever ready to promote good, who, living in an age of "Shoddy shams" is keen to discern and to probe —"the good phpsician and healer," whose heart and purse, which the "Elephant has stepped on," is ever open to the destitute and needy, I am proud to acknowledge as the helper in this as in every other act of my life by tendencies ever Upward and Onward!

THE AUTHOR.

CONTENTS.

Order of Poems—When Written.

*NOTES ON POEMS, ETC., ETC.

* Poems bearing dates are the author's.